WHERE ROSES FALL

A WINTER ROSE STORY

Jennifer Donnelly

Wild Rumpus Books
New York

WHERE ROSES FALL

www.jenniferdonnelly.com

Cover Design: Rochelle Bolima

First Edition, August 2024

ISBN: 979-8-9886471-4-0

For Douglas, my partner in crime.

Where Roses Fall

A Winter Rose Story

Prologue

Whitechapel, August 1900

No one could make Jimmy Evans cry.

His teacher couldn't, not even when she shamed him for being dirty.

Mel couldn't, not even when him and his pack of toughs laughed at Jimmy's raggedy jacket.

His father couldn't, not even when his belt buckle tore the skin off Jimmy's back.

Crying was for children. Jimmy was fourteen, and a man now.

Someone had to be.

His mum was dead since three weeks and his dad was a useless tosser and there were days when the hunger got so bad, he felt it would turn him inside out. Him and Ollie, they could take it, but Alfie cried so.

He'd gone to the market a few hours ago, as the costers were packing up for the night, and had scraped three smashed apples off the cobbles, pulled two wrinkled potatoes out of the gutter, and gathered up a handful of bruised cabbage leaves. He'd hurried home with his gleanings and Ollie had boiled them into a soup, doling it out by the teacupful. Alfie needed something hot. He was as pale as chalk and off his food.

It was Alfie he thought of now as he stared up at the old

factory's fourth-floor loophole, trying to work up his nerve. He thought of the baby's thin limbs and the dullness in his eyes, but it was the memory of the whimpers Alfie made, after yet another fit of coughing, that got him moving.

With a wary glance up and down the dark street, Jimmy started to climb. Hands wedged in behind the heavy downpipe in front of him, feet flat against the sooty brick wall, he pulled himself up step by hard, slow step. In only minutes, every muscle in his body was on fire.

Jimmy gritted his teeth against the pain and kept climbing, above the ground floor to the first floor, then the second. All he had to do was get up to the fourth floor, then step onto the window ledge, which was about two feet to the right of the drainpipe. He wouldn't be able to crawl into the factory through the window—its metal panes were too small, but the glass was gone in many of them, and he could hold onto the mullions as he made his way across the ledge. It was the loophole he needed to get to, on the far side of the window. It had a pair of metal shutters. The hinge was broken on one of them and the shutter was sagging open. Only a little, but a little was enough.

He kept his eyes trained above him, but as he climbed past the third-floor window, he foolishly glanced down and the street rushed up at him, whirling like a pinwheel. The sickening dizziness clawed at him, threatening to tear him off the downpipe. He closed his eyes against it and visions flashed through his mind. Of his body arching through the air. Of his skull smashing on the cobbles. And his courage trickled away like piss down a drain.

"Tosser," he hissed, banging his forehead against the pipe. "Get hold of yourself!"

They needed food. Medicine for Alfie. The landlord wanted his back rent. The basement room they lived in was dark and damp, but it kept them together and Jimmy knew that if they lost it, they'd be taken to the workhouse and split up. He and

Ollie could survive it, but Alfie wouldn't last a week.

He took a few deep breaths, then forced himself to open his eyes and keep climbing. A few minutes later, he reached the fourth floor.

"Now comes the hard part," he whispered.

A shallow flange, where one length of pipe fitted into another, sat parallel with the window ledge. Jimmy climbed up past the flange, then placed his toes on its lip, his left hand still wedged behind the pipe. When he'd steadied himself, he slowly stretched his right leg toward the window. His foot found the stone ledge. His reaching right hand closed on a mullion.

Quick as a cat, he released the downpipe and pivoted his weight sideways. And then he was standing fully on the ledge, with only a few thin, rusted pieces of metal to keep him there.

His heart crashed against his ribs like a trapped animal. "Keep your head…keep your bloody head," he whispered.

Jimmy forced his gaze to the right. There was an iron safety bracket bolted to the wall next to the loophole. *Same as before,* he thought. *Just get a foot onto the loophole's deck, reach for the bracket, transfer your weight.* But the gap between the window ledge and the deck was wider than the one between the pipe and the ledge. It had to be a good yard, and never had a yard seemed more like a mile.

"Don't think. Just do it," he told himself. He quickly stepped across the gap. His foot landed on the deck; his hand grasped the bracket.

And that's when he heard them—footsteps, heavy and rhythmic, echoing down the narrow street.

Jimmy froze. His hand tightened on the bracket. Slowly, he turned his head and looked down.

A man emerged from the darkness. He was carrying a bullseye lantern; its rays washed the cobblestones ahead of him in silver light. He stopped in front of a warehouse and tried its door. Then he raised the lantern and peered into one of its windows. Light bounced back at him off the glass. Jimmy saw it glint off the row of gold buttons running down the man's jacket and his guts turned to water.

The police constable lowered his lantern and continued down the street, testing a lock, rattling a chain. Jimmy remained motionless, one leg stretched across the gap, the other still on the shallow window ledge. He didn't dare shift his weight to the deck; it was old and made of wood, it would creak.

Closer and closer the constable came, until he was directly below Jimmy, rattling the padlock on the factory's door. All he had to do was shine his lantern up the wall and Jimmy was done for. But instead, the bobby put his lantern on the ground and pulled a small brass case from his jacket pocket. He clicked it open, drew a cigarette from it, then squatted down by the lantern to light it.

Jimmy's fear grew. How long was the man going to stay there? He could see the glowing tip of his cigarette now. He could smell the smoke.

Go, rozzer, Jimmy silently urged him. *Move on.*

But the bobby took his time, relishing each deep draw.

The cramp began slowly, just a soft, dark ripple through Jimmy's left leg, like a snake slithering through water. Then it wound itself tightly around the muscles of his calf and squeezed, harder and harder, until the breath left his lungs and sweat beaded on his skin and he bit his lip so hard, his teeth drew blood.

His body shook with pain, but he did not utter a sound. And finally, almost ten minutes later, the constable stood, threw the still-glowing stub of his cigarette onto the cobbles, and ground it out with the toe of his boot. Then he made his way down the rest of the street, still checking doors and windows, until he finally reached the bottom.

As he turned the corner, Jimmy drew a ragged sigh of

relief and lifted his other foot onto the deck, taking the weight off his cramping leg at last. The old wood creaked loudly, just as he'd known it would, but there was no one else there now to hear it. Little by little, the pain subsided. When it was gone, he wiped the sweat off his face with his sleeve. He had to get moving; the man had cost him too much time.

"Almost there," he whispered. "Almost in."

The loophole's deck was deeper than the window ledge, and Jimmy had room to turn his body around and flatten his back against the latched metal shutter so that he could brace his hands against the partly open one and push.

The metal gave a few inches, groaning as it did. The sagging shutter's top hinge was broken; its bottom edge had sunk into the deck. Jimmy swore at the noise, then pushed again until he'd opened up a foot-wide gap. He was as thin as a knife and squeezed through it easily.

The factory was dark inside, but Jimmy had come prepared. He pulled a stubby length of candle and a small box of Vestas from his jacket pocket. Fear had put a tremble in his hands, and it took a few tries before he was able to spark a match, then hold its flame to the candle.

As the wick caught, illuminating the cavernous room and its high vaulted ceiling, Jimmy stood in stunned disbelief, amazed that he'd actually made it inside. Then he hurried down several rickety flights of stairs, one hand cupped protectively around the candle. When he reached the ground floor, he wove past buckets of glue and grout, crated bathtubs, wheelbarrows, old jam jars filled with nails and screws, and boxes of tile, frantically searching.

"Where the hell are you?" he said, his nerves making his voice louder than it should be. He'd seen deliverymen unload them Friday morning as he'd walked past the factory.

Holding his candle high, Jimmy stopped in the center of

the room and turned in a slow circle. His gaze ricocheted off walls and corners; it hit the staircase, then sharpened. Something was underneath the stairs, covered by a paint-splattered tarpaulin. He raced back across the room, grabbed the tarp, and yanked it. As it fell to the floor, Jimmy caught his breath. At least thirty wooden boxes of new brass fittings were nestled under the stairs. Guilt, writhing like a maggot, burrowed deep into his heart as he opened one of them and lifted a shiny faucet out of it. He'd heard that a doctor had bought this place, a lady doctor. And that she was going to make a hospital out of it for poor people. People like him.

You're going to hell, Jimmy Evans, his conscience said. *You're going to the fiery depths where demons live and you get a good hiding and it smells bad.*

"Sounds just like Whitechapel," Jimmy countered. "Only warmer."

You're a thief now, Jimmy. Stealing from a doctor. What would your mum say? It'd break her heart.

"Shut it!" Jimmy shouted.

Alfie was sick and Jimmy knew his baby brother would die if he didn't find a way to get some money. What good would a bloody hospital do him then?

Jimmy grabbed a jam jar, dumped the nails out of it, placed his candle stub in it, and put it down on a stair tread. Then he reached inside his shirt and pulled out two folded flour sacks. He put one inside the other for strength, then stuffed the bag with faucets, taps, switch plates, and locksets. When it was full, he knotted the top and replaced the tarp. All he needed now was a coil of rope. After a quick search, he found one and looped it over his shoulder. Then he leaned down, grabbed the heavy bag, and heaved it onto his back. His legs shuddered under the weight, but he held the bag in place with one hand, picked up his candle with the other, and willed himself, step by staggering step, back up the stairs to the fourth floor.

He was panting by the time he reached the open loophole. Sweat was running down his face. He put the sack down, and the candle, then shrugged the coil of rope off his shoulder. Working fast, he wound one end of the rope around the neck of the sack and tied it off. Then he pushed the loose loophole door wide open and glanced up and down the street. It was empty.

"Thank Christ," he whispered.

Jimmy grasped the rope firmly in both hands, then nudged the sack toward the edge of the loophole's deck with his foot, hoping to ease the bottom free then bump the side over the edge gradually, giving himself time to take the weight. But the sack was hard to control. The top pitched one way, the bottom another. Jimmy nudged it again. It listed sideways, rolled forward, and toppled off the deck.

The sudden force against the rope jerked him forward. He screamed, but managed to slam his right hand flat against the closed loophole shutter, catching himself. He was holding the rope with only his left hand now, and it felt as if the weight at the end of it would rip his arm off. He almost pissed his pants with the agony of it. He almost lost his nerve. He almost let go of the rope and let the sack fall and smash everything inside it to bits. But then he saw Ollie in his mind's eye, holding Alfie through the long, sleepless night. Rocking him. Soothing him. Trying to make him better with no money, no help, no hope. They'd lost everything, the three of them. All they had left was each other. He'd be damned if they'd lose that, too.

With a deep groan, Jimmy got his weight back into his legs. Then, very slowly, he took his hand off the shutter and placed it back on the rope. His left shoulder throbbed, but he ignored it and let the rope out, foot by foot, until he felt it go slack and heard a clunk carry up from the street.

A jittery excitement coursed through him as he tossed the

end of the rope down. He was so close now, nearly in the clear, but things had almost gone badly wrong and they still could. He had to finish this. He had to get down and get gone.

He huffed his candle out and slid the jam jar behind a box. Then he stepped out on the ledge, pushed the unlatched shutter almost closed, just as he'd found it, and started his climb down. The ache in his shoulder slowed him. When his feet hit the ground again, he didn't waste time unknotting the rope from the sack, but gathered it up and took it with him.

Fear made him run. It chased him down the dark streets and the narrow alleys. Fear of bumping into another bobby or a gang of yobs who would beat him silly and take his hard-won loot. Fear that it was all for nothing, that he was too bloody late.

Jimmy tried to pray as he ran, but couldn't. He'd prayed for his father to stop drinking. He'd prayed for his mother to live. On days when the hunger gnawed like a wolf, he prayed for a piece of bread. But no one ever answered.

Words came anyway now—not a prayer, but a plea, his voice breaking as he uttered them, and no one to hear them but the hard London night.

"Hang on, Alfie. Hang on, little lad. Please, please, please hang on."

Chapter 1

He saw her from the window.

Her head was down, her face obscured by the brim of her hat, as she alighted from a hackney cab in a swirl of skirts and hurried toward the gaslit glow of the hotel's entrance.

Go. Now. Leave this place, a voice inside him said.

He could make it if he hurried. Out of these rooms, down the stairs, and through the back door.

It was what a good man would've done. But he was not a good man.

And so he stopped halfway across the room, hands clenched. Because he loved her. Because he wanted her. Like he'd never wanted any woman in his life.

He pictured her as she made her way through the lobby, still crowded late on a Sunday night with commercial travelers and their suitcases of samples, tweedy dons down from Cambridge, and young wives in from the eastern counties to buy their fall frocks.

This place, the Great Eastern Hotel—it wasn't what he wanted. He'd chosen it because it was bustling and anonymous, which lessened the chances of anyone noticing him. But people still did and that wasn't good.

The desk clerk noticed his knuckles, scraped raw from a

brawl in a whorehouse. He noticed his thick auburn hair, bound in a ponytail. He noticed his working man's attire, his powerful build, his arresting green eyes. Then the clerk noticed the ten pound note he'd quietly pushed across the marble counter and promptly forgot it all.

He wanted to take her away. The first time they'd made love, just a few nights ago in his room over the Barkentine, he'd vowed to take her to the sea, but she couldn't go. There were patients to see. He wanted to take her far from East London, from villains and their dark doings, to a place that was safe and all their own. If only he knew where it was.

The faint ping of the lift arriving echoed down the corridor, pulling the man from his thoughts. He heard footsteps in the hallway, light and eager, and felt his heartbeat quicken from happiness. And fear.

She scared him. He'd had plenty of women before her, and he'd given each one many things—money and jewels, clothing, furs. But he'd never given any woman his heart.

Until now. Until her.

Everything came with a price. What would this love cost them?

A knock came, a soft staccato. The man took a deep breath. He would do the right thing. He would tell her that this could not go on. He would end it.

And then he opened the door and the words he had planned to say fell away.

The woman took her hat off. She raised her eyes to his and it was not their cool gray beauty that made him catch his breath, but the silvery fire he glimpsed beneath it. She was like a river in winter, sparkling and alive beneath a mantle of ice.

As he stood there, desperate to go, aching to stay, feeling as if he would tear himself in two, she tilted her face to his and kissed him. Her lips on his, full of heat and desire, undid him.

Had he thought her a river under ice? He was the one who was melting. He pulled her across the threshold and into his arms. The door closed softly behind her. Her hat fell to the floor.

After a moment, she broke the kiss. "Hello, Mr. Malone," she said.

He leaned his forehead against hers and whispered her name. "India." He paused, then said, "I didn't know if you would come."

"Neither did I."

"But you're here."

"I shouldn't be," he said, pulling away from her.

Confusion darkened India's eyes. "Sid, is there something—"

Wrong, she was about to ask, but he didn't let her.

"Are you hungry?" he brusquely cut in. "I ordered room service."

He took her coat and hung it away. Then he led her out of the vestibule and into the suite's main room. A dining table stood in the center of it, set for two with white linens, glittering crystal, and flickering candles. Atop it were several silver-cloched plates.

"How about a glass of champagne?" he asked, pointing at a silver ice bucket. "Or a glass of Montrachet? There's a Bordeaux, too…Château Lafite, '72."

India inclined her head, smiling with amusement. "I had no idea you were a wine connoisseur."

"I'm not. The bloke in the penguin suit who brought them up is. Sit down. Eat," he said, pulling out a chair. "There's filet…" He lifted a cloche.

"Why did you order so many things?" India asked, her gaze skimming the table.

"I don't know what you like. Besides porridge. And that wasn't on the menu."

"That's very funny, Sid."

"You should eat something. You're too thin."

He picked up a knife and fork, cut a piece of filet, pushed it through the bearnaise sauce puddled on the plate, and held it out to her. But India shook her head.

"All right, then. I'll eat it," he said. "If you had to eat Desi Shaw's cooking, you'd jump at a nice bite of filet." He popped the piece of beef into his mouth, chewed, and swallowed it. "Look," he said, raising another cloche. "Duck. I think there's salmon as well," he added, frowning. "Somewhere under one of these bloody things. Christ, it's like playing the shell game."

He was talking too much, but he couldn't stop himself. India walked up to him, took the fork and the cloche from him, and put them on the table.

"I don't want any food. I want *you,* Sid."

She reached out then, to cup his cheek with her hand, but he caught her wrist, stopping her.

"Do you?" he said, a sudden flood of emotion making his words harsh. "Do you really? For fuck's sake, India, you don't even know me."

India, stricken, shook free of his grasp. She searched his eyes, trying—he imagined—to fathom a reason for his behavior, but he looked away. There were things, things deep down inside, that he didn't want her to see.

"What's going on, Sid? What's wrong?" she asked.

"Bloody everything, that's what's wrong. This. Me and you." He closed his eyes, hating his helplessness. "What the hell are we doing?"

"Falling in love," India replied.

Sid shook his head. "You are good, India. So bloody good. You don't deserve this. Meeting the likes of me after dark in some poxy hotel. Ducking into the lift, hoping no one sees you..."

"Look at me, Sid. *Look* at me," India said, taking his face in her strong healer's hands.

At her touch, his fear grew. He had to resist her. If he didn't, she would have him, all of him. Even the things he did not want to give her.

"I *do* know you," she said, her voice fierce now. "You are the man who took me on a tour of Whitechapel one night and introduced me to my patients. Do you remember?"

He did. How he wished to God that he'd never done it.

"You are the man—"

"Who robs warehouses for a living," Sid cut in, opening his eyes, but still refusing to meet her gaze. "The man who cracks safes and cracks heads. The man who runs guns. And gambling rings. And whorehouses."

"The man who gave money to a struggling mother to feed her children without taking her pride in return," India countered. "The man who gave a homeless woman his jacket, and a headstrong doctor ten thousand pounds to turn an old factory into a clinic for the poor. I know you, Sid Malone. And I love you."

Like a spooked horse, Sid pulled free of her, but she did not give up.

"And you love me. You told me so. In your room. In your bed. Was that a lie?"

Regret, as sharp as a straight-razor, sliced across Sid's face at her words. "If I loved you, I wouldn't be here," he said. "If I loved you, I'd let you walk away. If I loved you, I'd put a stop to this. I tried, India. I tried to not come tonight. I tried to figure out a way to tell you good-bye. But I don't know how. I don't bloody know how."

India took his hand. She pulled him after her through the suite of rooms to the bedroom, and Sid felt his resistance crumbling with every step. Once there, she pushed his jacket off his shoulders, then undid his vest and shirt, pressing her lips to his cheek, his neck, his chest. She kicked off her shoes, then unbuttoned her waistcoat, her blouse, the waistband of her skirt, her underthings, leaving a pile of clothing on the floor. She pulled the pins from the neat coil at the nape of her neck, and her blond curls tumbled around her shoulders.

"My God, but you're beautiful," he whispered.

She pulled him down on the bed with her.

"This is madness, India."

"Love is not madness, Sid," she said as they lay facing each other. "The time without you…the minutes and hours and days that I spend missing you and wanting you, *that* is madness."

He looked at her then, meeting her frank, demanding gaze, his eyes no longer hidden, their emerald depths revealing his love for her, and his longing. Revealing what it cost him to show her these things.

"We will find a way, Sid, you and I. We *will.*"

Sid laughed. It was a dry, joyless sound. "How, India?" he asked, brushing a tendril of blond hair out of her face. "It's impossible."

India stopped his words with a kiss. Gently, she pulled him to her. The warmth of her skin as she fitted herself to him, breasts and belly and hips, overwhelmed him.

"Make love to me, Sid Malone. I want you so," she whispered.

His desire for her became a deep, ferocious hunger. The more he filled himself with her, with the smell and taste and feel of her, the more he wanted. He covered her body with his own, parting her legs, opening her to him, making her his own.

But he was the one who surrendered. Since the night he'd first kissed her, in her flat on Bedford Square, he'd feared that his love for her would engulf him.

Now he knew it would. And he welcomed it.

Let me burn. Let me freeze, he thought.
Let the silver waters pull me under the ice.
Let me drown.

Chapter 2

It was the sounds that woke her.

A coster crying his wares. Dray horses clopping over the cobblestones. Pigeons cooing on the rooftop.

But it was the smells of the Whitechapel morning that made India Selwyn Jones open her eyes and smile. Onions frying on the stove downstairs. Chickens roasting in the oven. Apple cake cooling on the table. Coal smoke and horses.

All summer long, she had sweltered in the Moskowitzes' attic, tossing and turning in the heat, her nightgown sticking to her skin, but this morning a late August breeze lifted the window's faded curtains, carrying with it the promise of cooler days, of market stalls piled high with red pippins and speckled pears, and chestnuts roasting in braziers on street corners.

Dawn was breaking and India knew she should be out of bed and dressed by now; she had a busy Monday ahead of her. Instead, she pulled the worn quilt up around her neck and burrowed into her pillow, wanting to hold onto the morning's peacefulness for just a moment longer before the bustle and crush of the day snatched it away. Wanting to hold onto the memory of last night. Wanting to hold onto Sid.

But already she felt him slipping away. The feel of him, his scent, the sound of his voice—they were fading like stars in the dawn sky.

Their lovemaking had been hot and hard and over too quickly. She'd fallen asleep afterward, cradled in his strong arms, her head resting on his chest. But when she woke, she'd found herself alone in the bed.

Sid had put his trousers on and was standing at the window in the darkness, watching the street. India heard the clip-clopping of a horse. *A lone cab,* she thought. *Or a private carriage.* Whatever it was, Sid's watchful eyes followed it and hardened.

"What is it?" she asked him.

He didn't answer her.

"Sid?"

He turned to her, his eyes wary and evasive. "Nothing, luv. Are you hungry now?" he asked, with a forced smile.

Only a short while earlier, he'd gazed into her eyes as he'd made love to her and had given her a glimpse of their depths. But now those depths were hidden again, and it felt to her as if a shutter had closed, battened fast against a coming storm.

Sid didn't wait for an answer to his question; he padded out of the bedroom in his bare feet and returned a moment later with a bottle of red wine and two glasses. India drew the sheet up around her body. As he poured the wine, she propped herself up on one elbow, watching the candlelight play over him, drinking in the planes and angles of his face, the broad span of his shoulders, his powerful arms, the ripple of muscles down his abdomen.

He handed her a glass and she gulped the wine down as if it were water.

"Steady on, Missus," he said, putting the bottle down. "That's the good stuff. Cost me a bundle."

India licked wine off her lips, then held out her glass for a refill.

"Don't you think you should eat something first?" Sid asked, hands on his hips. "It's not wise to drink on an empty stomach."

India laughed in disbelief. "Are you scolding me?"

"Yes," he said, walking back out to the linen-draped table. "I am."

He returned with a plate of duckling, cutlery, and napkins and set it all down on top of the covers. Then he sat down next to her, sliced into the duck breast, and held out a piece to her.

"Here…it'll soak up the booze you just guzzled," he said.

India ate that bite, and a few more, and then discovered she was actually quite hungry. As she finished the duckling, a church clock struck the hour—midnight. Each chime felt like a blow to her heart. How had the hours passed so quickly?

"I have to leave," she said with a sigh, rising from the bed. "I have to go to the market early tomorrow to buy oranges."

"Oranges?"

"Yes. I'm giving them to children at the clinic. To help fight scurvy," she explained. "And I'm trying to convince their mothers to buy them. But when it's a choice between the landlord or the greengrocer, the landlord always wins. After I finish at the market, I'm off to meet with the builders."

"How's the renovation coming along?"

"Slowly," India replied, picking her chemise up off the floor and slipping it over her head. "But we're making progress. All because of you, Sid. Thank you."

He waved her thanks away as if the ten thousand pounds he'd given her to build her clinic were nothing, when they were everything.

A few weeks ago, she and Ella had lost their positions at Dr. Edwin Gifford's practice when they'd challenged the man over his callous treatment of his poor patients. Now they were building their own practice—seeing patients in an old shed in the Moskowitzes' backyard while using Sid's money to transform a decrepit factory on Gunthorpe Street into a modern, well-equipped clinic for the people of Whitechapel. At first, India hadn't wanted to take Sid's gift, deeming it blood-money made through his criminal activities. Right after she'd received it, she'd gone to his room, above the Barkentine pub in Limehouse, determined to give it back. Instead, she'd told him she loved him.

"The plumbing supplies arrived on Friday. *Finally!*" she continued, elatedly. "Tomorrow, the builders will start to install them."

Sid shook his head, smiling. "You're the only woman I know who gets excited about pipes and faucets."

"And toilets," India added. "They're even more exciting. I've twenty-four on order. All vitreous china with an improved germ-resistant, stain-proof finish. Which makes them so much easier to sanitize."

Sid made a face. India laughed at his reaction then picked up her blouse and threaded her arms through the sleeves. As she was buttoning it, he came up behind her and embraced her, crossing his arms over her chest, burying his face in her neck. They stood that way for a long moment, eyes closed, not talking, India melting into his warmth, feeling the rising and falling of his breath, the rhythm of his heartbeat.

And then he abruptly broke the embrace. "You go down first. Have the doorman call you a cab." He reached into his trouser pocket. "Here's money for the fare."

India refused it, preferring to pay the fare with her own money. "When will I see you again?" she asked him.

Sid hesitated, just for an instant, then said, "I don't know. It's hard to break away. I'll get word to you."

She nodded and finished dressing, and then she left, her head down, her hat brim over her face, hurrying through the hotel's lobby. Pushing the door open before the doorman could assist her. Disappearing into the night.

As she hailed a cab, she hadn't been able to shake the unsettling feeling that something had changed between them. From the moment she'd seen Sid standing tensely at the window, staring down at the street, it had felt to her as if a chill wind had blown in. She'd tried to reason with herself, putting his sudden strangeness down to the fact that this was all so new, that *they* were new.

And now, huddled under her covers in the Moskowitzes' attic, she closed her eyes and tried once more to shake off her creeping uneasiness, drawing on happier memories of their night together, picturing Sid's handsome face, his beautiful green eyes. Remembering the feeling of his lips on hers, his hands on her body...hearing his voice, whispering in her ear, telling her he loved her, saying her name...

"Ella! Ella and India! Miriam! Posy!"

India's eyes snapped open. That certainly wasn't Sid.

The voice, loud enough to wake all of Whitechapel, bellowed again. "Yankel, Aaron, Solomon!"

Across the room, Ella rolled onto her back in the old brass bed she shared with her sister, Miriam, and groaned, "*Gott im Himmel,* Mama!" Then she pulled the covers over her head.

Footsteps, purposeful and brisk, pounded up the attic's narrow wooden stairs, and then a woman was standing in the middle of the room, her white pinafore streaked with cinnamon and splotched with batter, her thick brown hair styled high on her head, her hands on her broad hips.

"Up now, children! There is much work to do this morning," said Sarah Moskowitz. "I have seen many things in my life, but I have yet to see a kugel cook itself!"

Chapter 3

"Mama, it's six o'clock in the *morning!*" Solly shouted, his voice carrying up to the attic from the floor below, where the Moskowitz boys slept.

"Yes, Solomon Moskowitz, it is!" Mrs. Moskowitz shouted down the stairs. "And where are you? Lolling about? Idleness begets much mischief!"

"I'm not *lolling,* Mama! I'm *asleep!*"

Mrs. Moskowitz turned back to her daughters and to India. "Does anyone know if there is a reason why Herschel Fein just deposited a mountain of oranges on my doorstep?" she asked.

Sid, India thought, remembering that she'd mentioned she needed them last night. Her heart warmed at his kindness.

"Because you ordered them?" Aaron yelled up the stairs.

"Don't be so fresh, *pisher!*" Mrs. Moskowitz yelled back. "I think I would remember if I had ordered fifty crates of oranges!"

Ella sat up in bed, the springs creaking underneath her. "Fifty crates, Mama?" she shouted. "There must be some mistake!"

In the Moskowitz household, shouting was the same as talking, India had learned, just a little louder.

"Herschel Fein assures me there is no mistake," said Mrs.

Moskowitz, lowering her voice slightly as she sat down on the edge of Ella's bed. "He says they were sent as a gift, but as for who sent them, he is not at liberty to say."

"Not at liberty to say?" Ella echoed, with a snort. "Is Herschel Fein a member of Her Majesty's secret service now?"

"Herschel Fein is putting on airs and graces, it's true. Ever since he married Moishe the bagel man's girl. She's too good for him and everyone knows it, but better the wife of a costermonger with ideas above his station than an *alteh moid,* I always say," said Mrs. Moskowitz, giving Ella a pointed look.

"I'm *not* an old maid, mama," said Ella, returning the look.

"Not yet."

"India's an old maid," Posy said, blinking sleepily from her own bed.

"Posy!" Ella scolded.

"She is! But not for much longer," Posy insisted, in a singsong voice. "She's going to get mar-ried! She's in lo-ove!"

"Oh, really?" Mrs. Moskowitz asked. "And who is the lucky man?"

"Sid Malone."

India froze. Fear skittered across her heart. She'd been so careful in public. She and Sid both. To never touch each other, to be careful of their words, to never reveal their true feelings. But they hadn't even managed to fool a child.

Then Ella said, *"Bist du meshugeh?"*

Posy sat up and glared at her sister. "I'm *not* crazy! It's true!"

"Pfft!" Mrs. Moskowitz said, flapping her hand. "What you don't see with your eyes, don't invent with your mouth."

"But I *did* see with my eyes, Mama!" Posy protested. "I saw Sid smile at India and I saw India smile back!"

Mrs. Moskowitz laughed, her dark eyes crinkling at their edges. "If a smile was all it took, *bubbelah,* I'd be engaged to Martin the *schnorrer*. He smiles at me all the time. Especially when I give him a slice of apple cake."

Posy giggled at that, and Mrs. Moskowitz rose and clapped her hands, clapping the sleep out of her children as if she were clapping pigeons out of her yard. "Hurry now, girls, and dress yourselves," she said. "There are potatoes to peel and chickens to pluck and fifty crates of oranges to bring inside."

India rose then, letting out a silent sigh of relief as she did. It was so impossible to imagine Dr. Selwyn Jones and Sid Malone together that Mrs. Moskowitz had immediately dismissed the mere idea. Her secret was still safe, but she would have to be more careful. If little Posy had glimpsed the feelings between herself and Sid, others might, too.

But as Posy and Miriam stood by the pitcher and basin on the dresser at the far end of the attic, bickering over who got to wash her face first, Ella walked up to India and caught her hand.

"Sid sent those oranges, didn't he? And that's where you went last night, wasn't it? To be with him. He's the friend you said you were going to see," she whispered. "*You* are crazy! Both of you!"

India's heart sank. Ella knew. "You and he are in agreement, it seems," she whispered back. "He also said that we were mad."

"I thought it was just a fleeting fancy on both your parts. The bad boy and the good girl. It's serious?"

India looked down at her hands. She nodded.

Ella let out a low whistle. "So..."

India's gaze lifted.

"Is he a good lover?" Ella asked, with a wicked grin.

"Ella!" India whisper-scolded, blushing.

"I'll take that as a yes," Ella said, then she went to take her turn at the wash basin.

As Ella walked away, India turned to make their bed. She didn't see her friend's smile fade or the light in her eyes darken.

She didn't see Ella glance back at her, frowning with worry, or hear her quietly say, "For God's sake, India, be careful."

Chapter 4

Olive Evans shook her head. Her hands came up to her mouth.

"Blimey, Jimmy! Where'd you get it all?" she whispered, her sleep-dazed eyes on the pile of food her brother had placed on their rickety table.

"Down the shops, where else?" Jimmy replied, tumbling lumps of coal into the grate.

It was half past seven now. He'd tried to be quiet as he'd set the food down and had begun to build a fire, but he'd still woken her.

"Where've you been?" she asked, turning to him.

"Got work, didn't I?"

"Where, Jimmy?" she pressed, tucking a tendril of lank blond hair behind her ear, worry on her wan face.

"Down the brewery, cleaning the vats. Getting 'em ready for the morning shift," Jimmy replied, with a cheery matter-of-factness.

But Ollie was unconvinced. "What's in that?" she asked, nodding at the flour sack resting on the floor.

"Some brass fittings the foreman was chucking in the rubbish. Should bring us a few bob."

Ollie winced. Jimmy saw the hurt in her blue eyes and

quickly looked away.

"Jimmy—"

"Give us the matches, will you?" Jimmy said, cutting her off.

"But Jimmy, Alfie's not—"

"Quick, Ollie, the matches. We need a fire. The cold's no good for him."

Ollie nodded. She looked as if she wanted to say more, but fetched the matches instead. Jimmy lied sometimes. When he had to. Never to her, though. But he didn't have a choice now. If the rozzers came calling about a robbery at a factory, he wanted her to be able to say she knew nothing about it and look as if she meant it.

He'd returned to their room just after midnight. Ollie had been sound asleep, worn out from tending to Alfie. She slept with the baby on their single bed, curled around him to keep him warm. Jimmy slept on a thin, dirty mattress that they rolled out at night. Alfie was a year old, and Ollie was only twelve, but she was a mother to him now.

Jimmy had put his heavy sack on the floor, then he'd sat down in their one chair, meaning to close his eyes for just a few minutes. He'd fallen asleep instantly and was startled awake at dawn by the sound of the tenant upstairs leaving for the docks.

He'd scrubbed the sleep from his face with his hands, then slipped out with the brass switch plates he'd nicked. Dan Boyle lived over his scrap yard and was happy to do business at any time of day.

A few minutes later, Jimmy was walking toward the High Street, trying not to run, the coins heavy in his pocket. As he'd made his way round the shops, his arms filling up with packages, he'd felt something kindle inside him, a feeling that was warm and bright. He hadn't been able to name it. As he tucked newspaper into the coal now and lit it, the feeling caught, too.

It grew, filling his chest as Ollie unwrapped the sausage rolls—half a dozen of them!—and gasped. As she touched the loaf of bread hesitantly, worried it might disappear under her fingers. As she saw the milk bottle, the tea in a twist of brown paper, the knob of butter and pot of jam. As she turned and smiled at him as if he were Father Christmas.

For one bloody moment in the whole bloody day, he could think of something other than the next meal. For one moment, he could stop the voice in his head that said it was all his fault—the hunger and the cold, the crying baby, the constant grinding fear. For one moment, he didn't have to see the shame on his sister's face as she asked the neighbor, yet again, to borrow a few pennies. For one moment, there was happiness in the cold, damp room.

Because of him.

Ollie threw her arms around his neck and hugged him tightly. "Thank you, Jimmy," she whispered.

The feeling inside him flared and burned bright, and suddenly he knew what it was. *Pride*.

"How's Alfie?" he asked as Ollie released him, eager to show the baby all the delicious food and get him close to the fire.

"He's...he's not well," Ollie said, worry returning to her face.

Dread knotted Jimmy's insides. "What do you mean?" he asked, his pride gone.

"I tried to tell you, but you wouldn't let me."

Jimmy was at the bed in a few quick strides. Alfie was lying on his back, his chest slowly rising and falling. His eyes, blue like Ollie's, like Jimmy's own, were open but unfocused. His face was pinched; his cheeks had a grayish cast.

"Hello, Sir Alfie!" Jimmy said, using his favorite nickname for the baby. "Who's a lovely boy?"

He picked the child up and held him close. Alfie usually

laughed and clapped when Jimmy held him, but all he did now was mewl. The dread inside Jimmy tipped into full-blown fear.

"He needs a doctor," Ollie said.

"No!" Jimmy shouted. Ollie flinched; her eyes filled with tears and Jimmy cursed himself. "*No,*" he said again, lowering his voice. "We can't go to a doctor. You know we can't. A doctor will ask questions. He'll find out that our mum's dead and our dad's gone and he'll put us in the workhouse." He took a steadying breath, then continued. "Alfie's hungry. That's all that's wrong with him. He hasn't had a proper meal for days. But we've got milk now. We can make him a nice warm sop with the bread. Maybe stir in a little jam." He jostled the baby playfully. "You'd like a bit of jam, wouldn't you, lad?"

The baby's eyes fluttered closed. His head lolled forward.

"Jimmy, I'm *scared,*" Ollie said, her voice breaking.

"Don't, Ollie. *Don't,*" Jimmy said through gritted teeth, knowing that if she broke down, he would, too, and crying was only for the rich. Poor people couldn't afford to cry; it took too much bloody time. "Get the pot…there you go," he said. "Now put it on the grate. Warm milk will put him right, you'll see. He'll be alright. He *will.* He'll be alright, Ollie. You'll see."

Chapter 5

Something was very wrong.

India knew it the moment she stepped inside the factory.

George MacNeil, her foreman, was standing by the staircase swearing at a pile of empty boxes. He was surrounded by his men, some with their arms crossed over their chests, others with their hands jammed deep in their trouser pockets. One held the stub of a lit cigarette in his palm, pinched between his thumb and forefinger.

"Mick, you can't smoke in here," India scolded, as she walked toward them, sidestepping a messy scattering of tool bags and lunch pails.

"Aw, Missus..."

"You'll thank me one day. At least, your lungs will," India added. Then she turned to her foreman. "George, what is it?" she asked, glancing down at the boxes. "Did something we need not arrive?"

George's eyes, bright with anger, met hers. "Got hit, Dr. Jones," he said, spitting the words.

"Hit?" India echoed, alarmed. Her eyes swept over him, searching for blood and bruises. "By whom? Are you hurt?"

"He means *robbed*, Missus," said Mick.

The words felt like a gut-punch; the shock of them took

India's breath away.

"When?" she asked, when she could speak again.

"Some time over the weekend," George replied.

"What was taken?"

"Faucets, switch plates...a lot of the new brass fittings. I sent one of my lads to fetch a constable."

India pressed a palm to her forehead, still unable to believe what had happened. After dressing in the Moskowitzes' attic, she'd hurried downstairs to help carry Sid's oranges through the café and into the back yard. Then she'd grabbed a still-warm bagel from a tray in the kitchen and had set off for the factory, eating as she walked, eager to meet with George and map out the next phase of the renovation, but her excitement had curdled, soured by the despicableness of the crime. She dreaded telling Ella.

"Those fittings were expensive, George," she said, "and now I'll have to buy them all again."

"What kind of tosser robs a hospital for poor people?" Mick muttered, shaking his head in disgust.

As he finished speaking, footsteps sounded in the doorway and a voice called out, "Good morning. Is there a George MacNeil here?"

India turned and saw a uniformed man, tall and broad-shouldered, with dark hair and brown eyes, walking toward them.

"I'm MacNeil," George said.

"Sergeant Roddy O'Meara," said the officer. He nodded at the lad who'd fetched him. "Your man here says a burglary occurred on the premises. Do you own these premises, Mr. MacNeil?"

"I do," India said, stepping forward. She introduced herself and explained her plans for the factory to the sergeant.

"Come on, lads," Mick said to his fellow builders,

motioning at a pile of lumber. "If we can't work on the plumbing, we'll work on the framing. The bastard who did this isn't going to slow us down."

"Who discovered the theft?" Sergeant O'Meara asked as the men bent to their work.

"I did," George said. "Didn't know anything was wrong 'til I got inside, about an hour ago. At first, everything looked just like it did when I locked up on Friday. No one had a go at the padlock. No one cut through the window mullions." He shrugged helplessly. "I can't figure it out for the life of me."

Sergeant O'Meara listened attentively, but his eyes were on the floor the whole time. "Is there another door to the building?" he asked.

"Yes, there's the rooftop door," India replied.

George shook his head. "Padlocked from the inside. I checked it."

"Who has the keys to the locks?"

"I do," said George.

His voice was tight, his hands were clenched. India knew what the sergeant was thinking—with no sign of forced entry, it appeared that whoever had robbed the factory had let himself inside it and George was the only one with the key.

She had hired George because Mrs. Moskowitz had recommended him. "He's as honest as the dawn," she'd said, and she was right: George MacNeil *was* an honest man, and India could see it pained him terribly that anyone might think otherwise.

"Mr. MacNeil is above suspicion, Sergeant," she said, coming to his defense.

"Yes, Dr. Jones, he is," Sergeant O'Meara agreed. "His feet are too big."

Surprise washed over George's face. And India's. "I beg your pardon?" she said.

Roddy pointed at the floor. India looked down, squinting

at the old pine planks, but could not fathom what it was he wanted her to see. There was nothing there. She looked up at him, questions on the tip of her tongue, but he was already across the room, pulling the tall wooden door all the way open.

Sunlight spilled across the floor as he did, and India saw what he meant her to: footprints, sooty and faint, looping back and forth across the floorboards from the staircase to the looted boxes. Her eyes swept from the prints back to George, and his feet, and she saw that Sergeant O'Meara was right—the footprints were made by smaller boots than George's.

"One of your loopholes has a broken metal shutter. That was the entry point."

"But that's impossible!" India exclaimed.

"It's all the way up on the fourth floor," George added. "And there's no fire escape, no ladder."

Sergeant O'Meara started for the staircase, motioning for India and George to follow him. As they climbed the steps, he pointed out more footprints. They ran in both directions.

"All the same size, same tread pattern," he observed. "One man was in here gathering the goods."

When they reached the fourth floor, Roddy led them to the loophole. They saw the shutter's broken hinge, and the freshly made groove its sagging edge had cut into the loophole's deck. O'Meara grasped the shutter's handle, lifted it up, and opened it all the way. Then, bracing one hand against the brick arch, he leaned out from the building and looked around.

"The downpipe," he said, as he came back inside. "He shimmied up it, stretched across to the loophole, then wedged himself inside."

"But how did he get out again with all the swag?" George asked.

"He had help," Roddy said. "There's no way one man could have done this alone. I'd guess there were three, maybe four of them—two lookouts at either end of the street, and one standing below the loophole, ready to take the goods. The inside man lowered them with a rope. It took careful planning. Guts, too. It's a long way down from here to the cobblestones. Whoever did it was a pro. Sid Malone's gang, I'd wager."

"No, Sergeant, it couldn't be," India said quickly. Too quickly.

Sergeant O'Meara caught the hastiness of her refutation. Though his face remained impassive, his eyes sharpened. "No? Why not?"

"Because Mr. Malone's generous donation is funding the factory's renovation," she explained. "Why would he rob it?"

O'Meara's eyebrows shot up. "Malone is paying for this clinic?" he asked in disbelief. "*Sid Malone?* I wouldn't peg him for a philanthropist."

"Have you met Mr. Malone, Sergeant?" India asked, bristling a little.

Sergeant O'Meara nodded, and India was surprised to see the ghost of a smile, small and sad, curve his lips. "Aye, a long time ago," he said.

Her curiosity piqued, she was about to ask him where, but before she could, he spoke again. "If you're right, Dr. Jones, things get a little more complicated."

"How so?"

"If it's not Malone's lads then it's a rival crew," Sergeant O'Meara explained. "One whose leader must be feeling bold."

"I don't follow you, Sergeant."

"He means The Firm don't take well to competition," George explained.

"Exactly," said Sergeant O'Meara. "There was a lad a few months ago—one of Teddy Ko's, another East London villain—who decided to add to his income by robbing one of Malone's… er…*colleagues.* A lady. One who runs an establishment of dubious—"

"A madam," India said flatly.

O'Meara colored slightly.

"I am a doctor, Sergeant," said India. "And syphilis is a disease."

"Yes. Well, as I was saying…this lad robbed a madam," the sergeant continued, "who works for The Firm. A day later, the lad was found floating in the river. After Frankie Betts—Malone's enforcer—was seen dragging him out of a pub."

A chill shuddered through India. She'd met Frankie Betts. Mad Frank, they called him. She remembered his swagger, his good looks, but above all, she remembered his cold predator's eyes. The thought that Frankie—an unstable, violent man—might involve himself or Sid in this unnerved her, but she tried to mask her worry. Sergeant O'Meara's penetrating gaze was on her again. Though she'd only just met him, she could see that he was smart, perceptive, and undoubtedly good at ferreting out the truth—and she didn't want to lead him too close to hers.

"Is there any hope of getting my belongings back?" she asked, changing the subject.

"I'm going to make the rounds of the pawnshops and the fences to see if any brass fittings have turned up," he replied. "I don't want to get your hopes up, Dr. Jones, but I'll do my best."

India thanked him, and then they all made their way back down to the ground floor. George rejoined his men and India walked Roddy O'Meara to the street. They said their goodbyes and the sergeant started off, but then he paused and looked up at the fourth-floor loophole.

India saw him. "Is there anything else I can help you with, Sergeant O'Meara?" she asked.

And then wished she had not.

For the sergeant shook his head grimly, and said, "It's not me who needs help, Dr. Jones. It's the lad who crawled up that pipe. Whoever he is, he better hope to God I find him before Sid Malone does."

❧ Chapter 6 ❧

Frankie Betts, standing with his back to the bar and a pint in his hand, gazed across the Queen Victoria at the small, bright-eyed terrier squirming in the arms of its owner. It was all the man could do to keep a grip on the animal.

"My money's on that one…Little Bill," Ozzie Briggs, another of Sid's men, said approvingly. "He don't even need to see the rats. Just the smell of 'em drives him wild."

"There's a few two-legged rats in this pub tonight as well," Frankie said, nodding at a sharply dressed man standing a few yards away. "What's Artie Chin doing here?"

"Betting on the dogs," Ozzie replied, pulling a silver cigarette case from his pocket. "Like everyone else."

"I doubt it, Oz. He's up to something."

Artie was Teddy Ko's right-hand man, and the opium trade had made both of them rich. Artie could afford to gamble in fancier premises than the Vic.

"Likes to place a bet, does Artie. Likes it maybe a little too much," Ozzie said, lighting a cigarette.

Frankie's ears pricked up at that. He liked to know other men's weaknesses. "Are you saying he has a problem?"

Ozzie gave a joyless laugh. He shook out his match and gestured at the room. "Every man in here has a problem, lad.

Look around. Who in his right mind would be standing in this shithole of a pub on a Wednesday night, or any bloody night, waiting for some toerag to open a bag of rats and set a dog on 'em if he didn't have a problem?"

Frankie's eyes roved over the room, taking in the battered faces, the mashed noses and torn ears, the missing teeth, the dead eyes.

Artie Chin and a few more of Ko's boys, all London-born Chinese, were sitting in one corner. Frankie knew most of them, and he knew they'd been scrapping since the day they were born. For money, like everyone else, but for more, too. For respect. For the right to walk down the street without being called names and told to go home.

Some of Billy Madden's boys were sitting in another corner, drunk and loud, gulping down pints as fast as Wilf, the publican, could pull them. One of them, Delroy Lawson, had been orphaned young and brought up in a workhouse, and had the scars to prove it.

Eliza Jeffries, the barmaid, had been thrown out of her home by her father when she'd fallen pregnant. She'd lost the baby soon after. She slept in the Vic after it closed, under a table, and ate scraps off the customers' plates. Wilf paid her well enough, but she spent every penny of her wages in the Limehouse opium dens.

"East London's made of problems," Ozzie said, motioning for a drink.

Frankie wanted to answer him back, but just as he opened his mouth, the rats were loosed in the ring, Little Bill was tossed in with them, and the evening's entertainment began. The punter's shouts, the crazed barking of the terriers outside of the ring, and the squeals of the terrified rats, drowned him out.

The ring-master was timing the dog with a gold pocket watch. Little Bill had sixty seconds to kill as many rats as he could. There would be a break when he finished, to pick up the carcasses, then it would be the next dog's turn.

As Frankie waited for Little Bill's minute to end, his eyes returned to Ozzie, bent-backed over his pint now. Anger rose in him, and contempt. There were lines in Ozzie's face, streaks of gray in his hair. It was time for him to call it a day. Find a nice little cottage in the country and plant some roses. Ozzie was the problem, the old misery-guts, not East London, not anyone else, and certainly not himself. He, Mad Frank Betts, had no problems. His father was dead, killed in a work accident, and his drunken slag of a mother had stumbled in front of a carriage years ago. But that was in the past. He had brass in one pocket now, and a revolver in the other.

He wasn't troubled a bit by the life and what it demanded—cracking heads, pimping, robbing—why should he be? What The Firm was doing in East London wasn't so different to what the toffs were doing in the West End. Them over there with their fancy townhouses and their country manors…they'd robbed to get their dosh, too. Frankie hadn't had much schooling, but he remembered stories about kings and queens, and he knew that as long as someone called you earl or duke or prince, you could take another man's treasure and his land, chop off heads, burn people at the stake, do whatever you bloody well liked. Well, he was a prince, too—a prince of the city. And he would take what *he* liked.

And if their king—his and Ozzie's and Ronnie's and all the other lads who worked for The Firm—was a bit distracted at the moment, well, it was probably because he was still recovering from the injury he'd gotten stealing guns from the Stronghold Wharf. Ripped his side wide open on a jagged piling when he fell into the river, Sid had. Almost died from the infection. That lady doctor had saved his life, and they were all grateful to her for it, but now she was taking liberties. She'd asked Sid to get her rubber johnnies for her patients, and just this past Monday, Sid had sent him, Frankie, to buy fifty flipping crates of oranges and get them delivered to her.

Sid was too good-hearted, wasting time on that harpy and her poxy clinic when his attention was needed elsewhere. Word had it that a load of valuable paintings was coming into London from Paris. They should be casing the warehouse where the shipment was headed, making plans, getting Joey Grizzard to line up a buyer. And what was Sid doing? Buying treats for kiddies.

Another shout rose as time was called and Little Bill, his muzzle dark with blood, was lifted out of the ring.

"Twelve rats in sixty seconds, gents!" the ring-master shouted. "A new record!"

Hurrahs went up. Another bag of squirming, squealing rats was deposited into the ring and a new dog was readied for his chance to unseat the champion.

Men, their glasses empty, bellied up to the bar during the break, shouting at Wilf for refills. Frankie, staring into his pint, still brooding, felt someone wedge in at his left. He turned his head and saw Artie Chin.

"Hello, Frankie. Quite the heist you lot pulled off on Gunthorpe Street," Artie said. "Which one of you climbed the pipe?"

Surprise got the better of Frankie. Confusion creased his brow. He had no idea what the bollocks was on about.

Artie blinked at him, equally confused by Frankie's puzzlement. But then a gleeful smile spread across his face. "Hang on a minute…you don't know anything about it, do you?"

Artie's words heated Frankie's simmering anger to a boil. He was angry at himself for allowing his ignorance to show, and angry at Artie for being so fucking smug. He took a sip of his porter and tried to keep a cool head.

"'Course I know," he said, licking foam from his lips.

Delroy Lawson, who was standing next to Artie now, had heard their exchange and didn't buy Frankie's feint at nonchalance.

"While you lot are tucked up in the Bark having tea and crumpets, someone's making off with the cream," he taunted.

Frankie's jaw tightened. His free hand knotted into a fist.

"Steady on, lad," Ozzie warned, watching Frankie in the mirror behind the bar.

"Mighty Marco! Mighty Marco's up next, lads!" the ring-master shouted.

"I wouldn't bet on him, Frankie. He's a loser," Artie said, still grinning. He patted Frankie on the back. "Just like you."

Then, pint in hand, Artie walked back to the action. Shame seared Frankie, making him feel stupid and small.

"Looks like all *Betts* are off," Delroy said, sniggering.

"Shut your gob, Del," Frankie growled.

"Blow me, Frankie."

The next thing the patrons of the Queen Victoria heard was a loud, resounding crack as Dell's head struck the bar. Frankie held it there, mercilessly mashing Del's face into the mahogany with one hand, holding a revolver to his temple with the other.

"Sure, Del, I'll blow you," he said, his eyes glittering. "I'll blow your brains right out of your thick skull."

Del, screaming and flailing, tried to shake him off. Then Frankie cocked the gun and Del froze, eyes wide, fingers clutching the edge of the bar.

"Fuck's sake, Frankie, I didn't mean nothin'!"

Frankie dug the muzzle deeper into Del's flesh. Del closed his eyes. Greasy sweat beaded on his brow.

"I told you once, lad...go easy," Ozzie said, taking a deep drag of his cigarette.

At the sound of Ozzie's voice, Frankie lifted his head and caught sight of himself in the bar's mirror. As his eyes met his reflection's, a look of naked hatred slashed across his face. He raised his revolver and fired. The mirror exploded. Men shouted and ducked. Jagged pieces of silver glass rained down. Ozzie blew out a lungful of smoke.

And Wilf, who'd dived to the floor the second he'd seen the gun, raised his head above the bar now like a soldier peering out of a foxhole.

"Christ, Frankie, what the hell have you done?" he shouted.

Frankie tucked the gun into his waistband. He reached into his pocket and pulled out a wad of cash. Several ten pound notes fluttered through the air and landed on the bar.

Ozzie, still watching him in what was left of the mirror, asked, "Is Artie wrong? Did we do it?"

"No, we bloody well didn't."

"Then who did?"

But all Ozzie got for an answer was the sound of the pub door slamming.

⁓ Chapter 7 ⁓

The blond showgirl, all lipstick and sequins, took a deep drag of her cigarette. "Auditioned for a part in a revue at the Lyric yesterday," she said, exhaling. "Director told me I'd have to shag him for it. For a bit part with two lines! Bastard never offers a girl a part, or even a bloody cab ride, without getting something in return."

"If you won't, there's plenty who will," said her friend, a brunette.

The blond made a face. "Have you seen him?"

"You're an actress, aren't you?" said the brunette. "So act."

"Excuse me, ladies," Sid Malone said as he edged by them, three dozen red roses nestled in the crook of his arm.

The showgirls were no more than eighteen or nineteen, he guessed, though the hardness in their eyes made them look older. They were standing backstage in a grimy hallway, leaning against a wall, but the minute they saw him they stood up straight. One cocked a hip; the other thrust her chest out. Both pasted diamond-bright smiles on their rouged faces, eyeing him like hungry strays eyeing a steak in a butcher shop.

Sid could smell them—cheap perfume, sweat, and the camphor they rubbed on their aching knees and feet. He knew all he had to do was give one of them a nod and she'd follow him into the nearest dressing room. He was a ticket out. Out of a shabby cold water flat. Off the casting couch. Away from the stage door johnnies with their lazy smiles and busy hands.

He doffed his cap and kept walking, moving past dressers carrying costumes, stagehands, musicians, until he finally reached the dressing room at the end of the hallway and knocked on the door.

"Come in!" a woman's voice trilled.

He turned the knob and pushed the door open.

"Hello, handsome," Gemma Dean purred, rising from her vanity table. "Are those for me?"

"Heard you brought the house down, Gem. Yet again," Sid said, handing her the flowers.

Gemma had a part in the Gaiety's new show. Sid had persuaded the director to cast her using a combination of money and muscle. She'd just finished the night's performance and was changing to go out with him for a late supper. Her hair was wrapped up in a scarf. A jar of cold cream stood open on the table. Crumpled rags, smudged with greasepaint, littered the area around it. A black silk kimono, embroidered with red flowers, covered her body. She put her flowers down and let the silky garment slip down her shoulders.

Once, just a glimpse of her corset, and her magnificent bosom foaming up over the top of it, would've had him as hard as steel; now it left him cold. Even as she pressed herself against him and whispered, "Fancy a bite of something sweet before supper?"

A laugh, throaty and low, drifted into the room. Sid had forgotten to close the dressing room door. Gemma's gaze slid away from him to the girls still standing in the hallway. Her expression darkened; her eyes flashed a warning. She reminded Sid of a lioness, older and battle-scarred, baring her teeth over a kill, warning off all young comers. The blond let her cigarette fall from her crimson-tipped fingers and ground it into the floor with her toe, but she didn't budge. Her stare was insolent. Her smile, slight and mocking, said that it was only a matter of time until it was all hers—the role, the roses, the rich, handsome villain.

Gemma strode to the door and slammed it shut, then she returned her attention to Sid. Pushing him down in a soft chair. Straddling him. Taking his cap off. Nuzzling his neck.

He didn't want this. He didn't want to be here, but he had to put in an appearance. It would raise suspicions if he suddenly refused to see her. You didn't end it with a woman like Gemma Dean for no reason. If he did, everyone would want to know what that reason was. Who it was. Until he could come up with a way out, he had to pretend he was all in.

But all the while, India beckoned to him. He could see her in his mind's eye with the sea sparkling behind her, a hand pressed to her hat to keep the salty breeze from snatching it away. It was where they belonged, the two of them, by the ocean. He felt this, knew this, deep down in his bones. Walking hand-in-hand, with the gulls wheeling overhead, and the sun shining down, and the rolling breakers washing every bad memory away, washing his soul clean.

But it was just a fantasy, a pretty dream. He'd walked too far down the road to perdition and there was no way back, no hope of redemption, not for him. He shook the pictures from his head now, and tried to figure out how he was going to get out of making love to Gemma. She was still undoing her corset laces, bending her head down to his, biting his lip. How would he explain it when he didn't…when he couldn't—

A sharp and sudden rapping startled them both.

Gemma sat up, a murderous expression on her face. "What's that bitch playing at now?" she muttered.

Thank Christ, Sid thought, as she closed her robe and

walked toward the doorway. The interruption would give him a minute to come up with a way out of this.

"What the hell do you want?" Gemma said, wrenching the door open.

"Evenin', Gem. Sorry for the bother, but I've got to see the guv. It's business, luv."

"Frankie?" Sid said.

In a heartbeat he was out of his chair and heading to the door, his relief replaced by dread. Why was Frankie here? The lad knew better than to interrupt him when he was with Gemma. With a glance up and down the hallway to make sure it was empty, he stepped outside of her room and closed the door.

"What is it?" he asked tersely.

"There was a robbery. A few days ago at the lady doctor's factory. Someone broke in and took what he could find...faucets, doorknobs, and the like."

A jolt of shock hit Sid at the boldness, the brazenness, the sheer suicidal nerve of it.

"Did Dr. Jones report it?" he asked, working to keep his voice steady.

"Aye, she did. It's O'Meara's case."

Sid's jaw tightened at the mention of the sergeant's name. He knew O'Meara. At least, he had known him. Long ago, in a different life. A better one.

"Who did it, Frankie?"

It was not a question; it was a demand. And Frankie heard it.

"We don't know, Guv," he said, shamefaced. "Not yet. But we will. I only found out about it an hour ago, but I've got all the lads out asking about it, and I went to see our dirty copper, the one on our payroll...Hughes. He gave me everything they have so far. He says O'Meara thinks a pro was behind it, a gang of 'em. I think so, too. No way one man pulled that off."

He told Sid how the factory had been robbed, and Sid could barely believe what he was hearing.

"Climbing up that high on an old drainpipe…who's mad enough to do that?" he asked. "And all for some brass fittings? It doesn't make any sense."

And then it did. And another emotion gripped him, squeezing the air from his lungs. It was one he'd boxed away years ago, one he barely recognized anymore. *Fear.*

"Billy Madden's behind it," he said.

"Could be," said Frankie. "Could be Teddy Ko, too. Max Moses. Charlie Walker. Whoever did it, it's a war he's wanting. No one steps on our turf like this for any other reason. This is the first shot over the bow."

"It's Madden," Sid said.

"How do you—"

Know, Frankie was going to say, but Sid cut him off.

"Because I do. You won't be able to get at Madden himself; he has too many men around him, so find the ones who actually did the robbing and bring them to me."

Frankie nodded, then started off down the hallway.

"Frankie!"

The lad turned back to him.

"Alive."

A sullen reluctance surfaced in Frankie's eyes at Sid's order, but he dipped his head and then he was gone.

Sid, alone in the hallway now, sagged back against the wall. He'd tried to push the fear he felt down, but it burst free, like a swollen river surging up its banks, overwhelming him.

Frankie was right; he'd read the writing on the wall—the break-in at India's factory *was* a declaration of war, but as usual, he hadn't read the fine print. Most crime bosses started a war gradually, nibbling at the edges of a rival's turf like a rat, shaking down small-time bookmakers, publicans, and madams under his protection; knocking off a shop or two; provoking his lads; planting cheats at his card games.

This man was taking a different tack. A darker one.

Brass taps and doorknobs were not bullion or banknotes or jewelry. They had some small value, but nowhere near enough to entice a major player to risk his neck. But Billy Madden hadn't done it for the dosh; he'd done it to send a message, one that only Sid could read, one that said he knew all about Sid Malone and the doctor.

But *how?* How had he found out?

Sid knew the answer, though he didn't want to admit it. He'd been worried about meeting India at the Great Eastern, but he'd gone anyway; he hadn't been able to help himself. After they'd made love, he'd gotten out of bed and had gone to the window. And that's when he'd seen him—Billy Madden—walking down the Great Eastern's steps and disappearing into a carriage.

Madden had followed him; he was watching him, Sid was certain of it. He was looking for something he could use against him, and he'd found it.

Sid closed his eyes, cursing himself. Long ago, he'd lost the ones he loved—his father, his mother, his infant sister—and the pain of those losses had been so great, he'd vowed never to let anyone into his heart again. But he'd broken that vow, and now India would pay for his recklessness.

Fury filled him, pushing his fear aside. Fury at Madden. Fury at himself. Sid felt it rising in him, closing his throat, beating at his skull. His right hand clenched. With a yell, he swung around and drove it into the wall. The plaster was old, the lath underneath it rotten. His fist went straight through them.

"Sid? What's going on?"

It was Gemma. She was standing out in the hallway, holding her robe closed. Her eyes widened in alarm as she saw his torn hand and the rubble of plaster and wood on the floor.

"I have to go," he said.

"But you're bleeding!" Gemma protested, reaching for him. "At least let me see to your hand."

Sid shook his head. "I'll be fine."

Hurt filled her eyes at his refusal of help and Sid's heart clenched. He didn't want to hurt her. He didn't want to hurt anyone, and yet he did, over and over again. He reached into his pocket with his good hand, drew out a few notes and gave them to her. "Treat the girls to supper. I'm sorry, Gem, I am. But this can't wait."

Out on the street, he shouted an address up at Ronnie, his driver, then climbed into his carriage. As it rolled through the dark streets, Sid sat back and closed his eyes, steeling himself for what he was about to do. He was used to villains coming after him; it was the way of things in his world. But Madden was breaking an unspoken rule. He was fighting dirty, using an innocent woman for leverage. He clearly didn't just want The Firm and its lucrative holdings; he wanted Sid himself, and would stop at nothing to get him.

What Madden didn't realize, though, was that he already had.

There were many ways to kill a man.

But if you wanted to kill him quick, there was only one: strike at his heart.

Chapter 8

A light was on, its golden glow illuminating the ground-floor windows of the old factory, making them shine like distant stars in the deep London night.

And alerting every criminal in London that she's in there, Sid thought. *Alone, most likely. At eleven o'clock at night on a deserted street.*

"Christ, India. Tell me you've got enough sense to have a proper lock on the door," he said, getting out of his carriage.

He told Ronnie to wait, then knocked on the door. A moment later he heard footsteps.

"Who is it, please?" a voice called out.

As if she's expecting the vicar, Sid thought.

"It's me, India. It's Sid," he said.

"Sid!"

There was the sound of a bolt sliding back, the door whined on its hinges, and then she was there, standing on the threshold, sleeves rolled up, a pinafore covering her clothing, blond curls scraped up in a loose knot, eyes sparkling behind her spectacles, lips curved in a beautiful smile.

At the sight of her, Sid's resolve almost crumbled.

"This is the most wonderful surprise," she said. "Come in."

"Is Ella with you?" Sid asked as he stepped inside.

"No, it's just me," India replied. "I'm going over the

blueprints. The builders have questions on the placement of the showers."

"You shouldn't be here alone, India," he said tersely. "Not at this hour. Not at any hour."

"Shouldn't I?" she asked, a mischievous note in her voice. "If Ella was here, I couldn't kiss you. And I very much want to."

She moved toward him and took his face in her hands. He felt her lips on his and everything in him—his body, his heart, his soul—strained toward her. Toward the light in her eyes, the heat in her kiss, the softness of her touch. He folded her into his arms, wanting to live in this moment with her forever.

Let her go, you selfish bastard, a voice inside him said.

He closed his eyes, letting himself taste her, feel her, remember her. And then he opened them, and did what he'd come to do. He stepped back from her. Breaking their kiss. Breaking his heart.

India's eyes searched his. He saw confusion in them and the first bright pinpricks of dread.

"Something's wrong, isn't it? That's why you're here. What is it, Sid?" she asked.

"I heard about the robbery."

India nodded, her worried expression easing a little. "Yes," she said. "They took quite a bit, I'm afraid. It's disheartening, but it's not the end of the world. No one was hurt. And Sergeant Roddy O'Meara, who's investigating the case, is hopeful that at least some of the stolen goods might be recovered. He thinks more than one person is involved. He thinks—"

"I know what he thinks, India."

India tilted her head. "How?" she asked. "Have you spoken with him?"

"It's my business to know what happens in East London."

"Right. Yes. On your turf," India said, looking down at her hands.

"It was a well-executed job, not some shabby smash-and-grab," Sid said. "The ones who did it, they're working for a big boy, for Billy Madden. He's the boss of west London, and he doesn't waste his time nicking faucets."

India raised her head. "Then why did he?"

"Because he knows about us. I think he saw me at Great Eastern, and then he saw you, and put two and two together," Sid said. "I think he followed me there. And probably paid the desk clerk more money to talk than I paid him to keep quiet."

India shrugged. "Why does it matter? Why would Mr. Madden care about me? You've had other lady friends. He hasn't gone after them, has he?"

"You're different and he knows it. You're too good, too kind. You're not ruthless, and you have to be to survive in my world. He knows that if he hurts you, he'll hurt me."

"*Hurt me?*" India echoed. "He wouldn't—"

"He *would*. He wants a war. And I've seen what's left when villains do battle. Lying in an old warehouse. Rotting in an alley. Floating in the Thames." He stopped pacing then, his gaze inward, and said, "He's going to pay for this. Dearly."

India swallowed hard, but kept her voice steady. "I'm not afraid of Mr. Madden. Or anyone else."

Sid rounded on her. "For God's sake, India, you should be!" he shouted. "I put you in danger. By being soft. By being stupid. I did it and now I need to undo it."

India went very still. "What does that mean, Sid?"

Sid didn't reply. He couldn't. But he didn't have to. India was not a fool.

She backed away, hands raised, as if trying to push away what was coming. "No. *No.* You're not…you're not breaking it off with me, Sid…say you aren't."

"I have no choice," Sid said, anguish tearing at his voice. "I love you, India, and that love is going to get you killed."

He expected anger. Harsh words. A slap. That's how all the other women he'd been with had responded when he ended things. But he didn't get them. Instead, tears welled in India's gray eyes, turning them silver. They spilled down her cheeks. The sight of those tears, the knowledge that they were his fault, nearly killed him.

"Don't cry...please don't cry. I'm not worth it."

"I-I gave you my heart, Sid. And now you want me to take it back. I don't know how. I don't know how to not love you."

"You'll find someone else. Someone better. This is for the best, can't you see that?"

"For the best?" India echoed. She tried to say more, but it took her a few tries before she could get the words out. "You are cruel, Sid Malone."

Sid had survived all of these years only by controlling his emotion and he'd become so good at it. Until now. Until this woman.

"Christ, India, do you think I want this?" he shouted.

At his outburst, she turned away from him, lowering her head into her hands.

"You are the brightest, most beautiful thing I have ever seen," he said to her. "You are goodness in a place starved for it. I won't be the one who destroys that." He went to her. "Look at me...look at me, India." He turned her to him, cupping her face with both of his hands, wiping her tears away with his thumbs. She raised her eyes to his, and the pain he saw in them made him wild with desperation. He needed it to stop. He needed her to understand why he was leaving her. "I have nothing, *nothing,* and I never will. I need to know that you're here. Safe. Keeping a light burning. Let me have that. *Please.*"

He kissed her forehead. Tears burned in his own eyes. He squeezed them shut, trying to hold in the pain of his shattered heart. And then he turned and walked away from her, from her brightness, her light, her love.

"Where to now, Guv?" Ronnie asked him, as he walked toward his carriage.

"Stay put. Wait for Dr. Jones and take her home."

Ronnie acknowledged Sid's orders with a dip of his head and then Sid was gone, walking down the crooked, cobbled street. Back to the night. Back to his world. Back to the life. It was darkness and destruction. It had taken hold of him years ago and it would never let him go, but he would not let it take her, too.

Frankie Betts was hunting for the ones who'd done the job and Frankie hunted like a panther—silently, stealthily, his prey unaware of what was coming until it was too late.

Billy Madden had sent Sid a message.

Now it was time to reply.

Chapter 9

"Who's a good boy, eh? There you go, Wellie lad. Get that down you. It'll put a shine on your coat."

The small fox terrier, standing on top of the shop's wooden counter, caught the chunk of liver Joe Grizzard tossed to him and gobbled it down. Grizzard smiled, sliced a few more pieces from the large slab lying on a square of butcher's paper, and tossed those to the dog, too. With each push of his knife, the liver wobbled like a glossy brown jelly.

Which made Jimmy Evans feel like his breakfast might come back up. For a moment, he wondered where the liver had come from. A cow, hopefully. But with Joe Grizzard, you never knew.

A barrel-chested man, with close-cropped salt-and-pepper hair, a brawler's nose, and hands barnacled with heavy gold rings, Grizzard had an imposing physical presence that made both the cops and the robbers think twice about causing him grief. Just last week he'd nearly pounded the face off a lad who'd tried to slip a silver fork off the shop's counter and up his sleeve. But Jimmy wasn't looking to rob him. He'd heard that Joe Grizzard paid fair prices for all manner of goods, not just the fancy stuff, and Jimmy didn't want to go back to Dan Boyle. Spreading the swag around made it harder for the coppers to trace it.

The boy clutched the bundle he was carrying, wrapped up in old newspaper, and started toward Grizzard. He had to pick his steps carefully. With teetering piles of clobber everywhere, and narrow paths snaking through them, the shop looked as if rabbits had tunneled through it.

A pram with no wheels, dolls with cracked faces, a rusty Tetley sign, chipped pudding molds…Jimmy moved carefully through all of it, worried he might bump something and bring an avalanche down on his head. Some people said Grizzard hoarded rubbish to make it look like he was nothing more than an old rag-and-bone man instead of East London's most notorious fence. Others said he hid things deep in those piles: silver and gold, jewels, guns. A body or two.

"Morning, Guv," Jimmy said, as he reached the counter. "You buy brass?"

The fox terrier looked up first, his nose twitching. Then Grizzard did. He was standing behind the counter. A small desk stood to his right. There was a doorway on his left, which was curtained off from the rest of the house.

"Don't believe I know you, lad."

"George Archer."

Grizzard cocked an eyebrow. "George Archer, is it? You don't trust me, George Archer, I don't trust you." He jerked his thumb toward the door.

Jimmy flushed, embarrassed at being caught in a lie. "Jimmy Evans," he said.

"Evans, eh? I know your father."

"Then you know he's a tosser."

"Where do you live, Jimmy Evans? So I can come after you if the cops come after me for whatever's in that parcel."

"Thrawl Street. Number Twenty-one," Jimmy said, setting the bundle down.

Grizzard opened it, then picked up the three faucets inside it one by one, inspecting them in the light of a dirty window.

"Where'd you get them?"

Jimmy hesitated.

"Tell me they fell off a wagon and I'll make you eat them."

"I robbed an old factory."

"Fifteen bob. All in."

Jimmy blinked at him in disbelief. "For all three? Them faucets go for a pound apiece! How about one and ten?"

Grizzard tossed Jimmy a look that said he was pushing it. "Sixteen bob. Take it or leave it."

Jimmy heaved a grudging sigh. "I'll take it."

He had no choice. He didn't have time to shop the goods around. Their landlord was going to throw them out in the street if Jimmy didn't get him the back rent by nine o'clock that morning, and Alfie needed medicine. The baby had rallied on Monday, after Ollie had fixed him a warm milk sop, and after she'd given him cough syrup that Jimmy had bought at the chemist's. He'd held steady for a few days, but last night he'd taken a bad turn again. Jimmy needed to find different medicine for him, better medicine. And he needed to do it now.

Grizzard opened a metal cash box and pulled out a handful of coins. He counted out Jimmy's payment and slid it across the counter.

"Ta very much," Jimmy said sarcastically, as he pocketed the money. Then he headed for the door.

Worried about getting to the landlord's in time, Jimmy didn't notice how Joe Grizzard's eyes followed him as he let himself out, or stayed on him as he walked past the shop window. He didn't see the curtains twitch in the doorway behind the counter, or a man, young and rangy, step out from behind them.

"Billy Madden's a cagey bastard, ain't he? Sending a kid

here. Telling him to say that *he* did the job," said Frankie Betts with a snort. "Rob a factory by himself…*that* skinny little gobshite? How stupid does he think we are?"

"Why are you so sure it's Madden?" Grizzard asked.

"I wasn't, but I am now. This move's got Big Billy written all over it," Frankie replied. "He's the cheapest bastard I've ever met. He should be smart and throw the swag in the river, but no, he's got to get his sixteen bob out of it."

"Penny wise and pound foolish," Grizzard said, cutting another slice of liver and tossing it to his dog.

"He'll pay. Swear to God he will. I'm going to find out which of his men did the job and then I'm going to do for them. I hope to God Delroy's mixed up in it. Nothing I'd love better than to throw his useless arse off Tower Bridge. Right after I throw that bloody kid's off." He shook his head, annoyed with himself. "I should've done for him right here."

"No, you shouldn't have. I don't want blood all over my floor. And don't you run out of here and grab him, either!" Grizzard said, his voice heated. "You know where he lives now. Go get him there. I don't want the cops nosin' around."

"All right, Griz. Calm yourself," Frankie said, holding his hands up. "I'll wait a bit. Get Ronnie to help me. Lad might put up a fight. Most of 'em do."

"Shame, really," said Grizzard. "Him being a kid an' all."

"It's on Madden," Frankie said with a shrug.

"You be careful now, Frankie," Grizzard warned, glancing up from the liver. "Villains scrappin' is bad for business. So's a dead kid floating in the Thames. You start a war, it'll bring the Yard down on us—*all* of us."

"Ta, Griz. I owe you," Frankie said. And then he was gone.

After the door had closed behind him, the fox terrier pawed at the butcher paper, whining.

"You're a greedy guts, Wellington," Joe Grizzard scolded.

"You don't know when enough's enough. Seems no one around here does."

His eyes were on the dog as he spoke, but his mind was elsewhere, and troubled. He folded the butcher paper around the remains of the liver, then came out from behind the counter. Fording his way through the piles of clobber, he walked to the shop's door and locked it.

"Wellie, lad," he said, making his way back to the dog, "how do you feel about visiting my sister Rosie up in Kentish Town? Someone's about to go for a swim. And when that happens, we all get wet."

Chapter 10

Lavender's blue, dilly dilly,
Lavender's green.
When you are king, dilly dilly,
I shall be Queen…

Ollie's voice broke on the last word of the pretty song. "Wake up, Alfie. Please wake up. *Please,*" she begged.

The baby's eyelids fluttered, but he did not stir. Ollie pressed her hands over her own eyes, trying to hold her tears back.

Ever since Monday, Jimmy had been saying that Alfie would get better, and he had for a bit. But now it was Thursday morning and he was sinking again. His little face was pinched. His lungs made frightening noises every time he took a breath. His forehead was burning hot.

Ollie was all alone with him. Jimmy had gone out. He'd pulled the sack out from under the bed earlier, taken faucets out of it, and wrapped them up in newspaper. He'd told her that he was going to the landlord's, and then the chemist's. Ollie had begged him to fetch a doctor instead, but he wouldn't hear of it.

"The chemist will know what's good for a cold, same as a doctor," he'd said.

Alfie had more than a cold, anyone could see that. And his

illness was sapping him. It had taken away his smile, his happy chatter, the pink in his cheeks. All he did now was lie on the bed, sometimes coughing, sometimes whimpering, sometimes lying so still that Ollie cried out in terror and shook him to make sure he was still alive.

As she watched her baby brother now, a new fit of coughing seized him, shaking his small body like a winter wind through bare branches. His eyes, open now, found hers. She saw the misery in them and sobs burst from her. She rubbed his back, trying to ease his pain, and all the while panic clawed at her. Finally, the fit eased and Alfie closed his eyes again, his breath coming in short, quick gasps.

Ollie wiped her tears away with the heel of her hand, leaving dirty smears on her cheeks. She'd tried so hard to take care of the baby, just as she'd promised her mum she would. She tried to be a grown-up and do the right things, but she didn't know how. She had watched her mum die in this very room. In the same bed Alfie was lying on. A doctor had come, but he hadn't done much besides talk.

Anemia...Abscess...Tuberculosis...

Ollie didn't know what his big words meant, but she knew her mum died because she was tired. Tired of trying to buy food with only a few pennies. Tired of shivering in their damp, cold room. Tired of the beatings. A lot of people died because they were tired. And now Alfie was tired. He didn't laugh anymore. He didn't clap his hands and chortle and try to pull himself up on the back of the chair. He didn't pull Ollie's face down to his and give her a noisy kiss.

A doctor could fix him; Ollie was sure of it. Not a careless one like her Mum had, making faces at the mold on the walls and the bugs on the ceiling, a good one. Ollie didn't know how to find a doctor, but she could ask a neighbor. She did know you had to pay a doctor, though, and she didn't have any money.

She wrapped her arms around herself, fingers digging into her sides. No matter how hard she tried to figure out a way forward, everything felt like a dead-end.

"What do I do? I don't know what to *do*," she said in the silence of the small room.

As if in answer, Alfie let out a high, anguished wail, then started coughing again. This time the fit did not pass quickly and Ollie watched helplessly, scalded by fear, as it racked his small body and stole his breath. She sat him up, but it didn't help. Frantic, she pulled him onto her lap. Rubbed his chest. Patted his back.

"Breathe, Alfie, like a good little man…breathe, Alf, just breathe," she sobbed, as he started to turn blue.

The coughing tore at the baby's throat. The awful blue tinge deepened. Alfie's eyes rolled back, and then, just as Ollie was sure she would lose him, there was a soft, sucking whoosh and his airway opened. His lungs filled, but he was exhausted and sagged in her arms. Weak with relief, Ollie laid him back on the bed.

That's when she saw it.

A smear of crimson across his mouth.

"No," she said, her heart battering against her ribs. *"No!"*

She fell to her knees by the bed, opened the sack, and grabbed the first thing she saw. As she stood, she snatched a dishcloth off the table and bundled the object up in it.

Seconds later, she was hurrying down the street, her arms around Alfie, the bundle clutched in one hand. She tried to walk at first, so that she didn't jostle the baby, but by the time she got to the end of the street, she was running.

Chapter 11

In an accent as thick as jam, the old woman said, "That's 'ow it is, Missus, innit? Them wot 'as nuffink will give you everyfink. An' them wot 'as everyfink will give you nuffink."

"But Mrs. Barnett, *you* have nothing," India said. "And you badly need the orange that you just gave away."

"The nipper needs it more."

India took a deep breath. "Mrs. Barnett, we now believe that a chemical compound within oranges can help cure bleeding gums, myalgia, bruising, and other ravages of scurvy."

Mrs. Barnett patted India's arm with a gnarled hand. "Do you, luv? That's nice. Me? I know wot it is to be 'ungry. Once you know that, you'd give whatever you 'ave to keep someone else from knowin' it."

"Admit defeat, Dr. Jones," said Ella, hurrying by them with a basket of dirty rags. "This is one battle you're not going to win."

But India would not, for she hated losing. Mrs. Barnett had come to the clinic complaining of fatigue and aching bones. After examining her, India had diagnosed scurvy. She's given the old woman an orange to help combat it and had instructed her to eat several of them a week. But as Mrs. Barnett had left, she'd handed the orange to a thin girl, perhaps six years old, who was sitting on an overturned tea crate with her mother, waiting to be seen.

India had grabbed another orange from a bowl and had hurried out of the old shed after her, apologizing to her waiting patients, telling them she'd be right back. She'd caught up with the old woman halfway across the Moskowitzes' yard.

"Please, Mrs. Barnett. Take this home and eat it. For me?" she said, putting the orange into the old woman's hands.

"All right, dearie," Mrs. Barnett said, reluctantly accepting India's offering. "If it makes you 'appy. Ta ra!"

And then she left, her orange in one hand, a prescription for a stronger solution of laudanum in her pocket. It was the best India could do for her.

Ella passed by again, this time with a basket of clean rags, just pulled off the clothesline.

"How many oranges do we have left?" India asked her.

"A few dozen," Ella called over her shoulder.

India let out a sigh. "We need a few million," she said, still gazing after Mrs. Barnett. The old woman was heading for the doorway in the brick wall at the bottom of the yard.

India noted her shuffling, side-to-side gait. Scurvy was only one of Mrs. Barnett's problems. Arthritis was another. Cataracts. Poor circulation. And a rattling cough.

As Mrs. Barnett reached the doorway, she stopped to lean against the old wooden frame, her gray head bowed, visibly struggling. India winced; she knew that her odd gait was caused by bone hitting bone in the joints of her knees and wondered how anyone in such pain could muster the courage to get out of bed in the morning, never mind smile and joke and give a precious orange away.

She was just about to turn around and walk back to the shed, when she saw Mrs. Barnett take a deep breath and raise her head. The withered hand resting against the doorframe knotted into a fist, then she continued on her way. And suddenly, hot, stinging tears were brimming in India's eyes. She looked up at the sky, trying frantically to blink them away, but it was no use; they slipped down her cheeks, shimmering silver rivulets of sorrow.

"Stop it…*stop!*" she hissed at herself.

Last night she'd promised herself she would not do this. She'd wept after Sid had left her. Standing alone in the old factory on Gunthorpe Street, she'd wept until her eyes were swollen and her throat was raw, and then she'd wiped her face on her sleeve and picked up her blueprints. She could not afford to fall apart; her patients needed her.

And she had kept her promise. Until now. Until Mrs. Barnett.

This place, this Whitechapel…it could be so harsh, so heart-breaking, yet its people were brave and resilient, defiant even. India saw their courage daily, in their smiles and laughter, in their refusal to give up, and in the kindnesses they showed one another, kindnesses that were often small and quiet, but so deep, they made her catch her breath.

India's heart had been shattered before, several times. Losing Hugh Mullins, a boy she'd loved and had meant to marry, had nearly killed her. Losing her beloved cousin Wish to suicide had plunged her into a deep grief. And discovering, earlier in the summer, that her fiancé, Freddie Lytton, had maliciously betrayed her, had upended her entire world. But Whitechapel had put that broken heart back together, piece by piece. A baby saved after a hard birth was one piece. A sick child cured was another. The Moskowitzes making room for her in their home and in their hearts. Her clinic. And a man, dangerous and difficult, whom she loved beyond reason. It had happened gradually, this mending of her heart, and almost against her will until all at once there it was, shining and whole, like a coin long buried in the river mud, slowly lapped bare.

And last night, the man who had helped mend her heart had broken it all over again.

"Crikey, India, it's only bloomin' oranges. We can get more."

India looked up. It was Ella. Carrying another basket of clean rags. She was staring at India in open-mouthed surprise.

"I'm sorry, Ella. Blast. Blast. *Blast.* I must stop. I *will* stop," India said, shaking her head at her foolish and self-indulgent behavior. "There are patients to see. There are always patients to see. And it's just the two of us. And we could use help. Another pair of hands. Or rather, ten pairs. My God, it's like trying to fight a war with a slingshot."

Ella put her basket down, grabbed India's arm, and pulled her behind the shed where no one could see them.

"This isn't about oranges, is it?" she said, giving her a searching look. "Or patients. Is it the robbery that has you so upset?"

India had told Ella about the theft of their supplies right after she'd learned of it herself, and Ella had been as crushed, and as angry, as India had been.

"In a way, yes," India replied. Then she told Ella what had happened between Sid and herself, and how Sid was convinced that one of his underworld rivals was behind the robbery, and that who'd ever done it might well hurt her, possibly even kill her, to get at him.

"Sid wanted me to understand that," she told her friend. "He wanted me to know that having him in my life might be the end of me. But there's something he doesn't understand, Ella—that not having him in my life will be the end of me, too."

And then she railed—between fresh, gulping sobs—about Sid's heartlessness, his cruelty. Ella put an arm around her and let her. And when her sobs had lessened a little, Ella gave her a clean rag from the basket.

"He was wrong to do it, Ella," India said miserably, wiping her eyes.

"No, India," Ella said gently. "He was right."

Ella's words felt like sharp stabs of betrayal. "How can you say that?" India asked, wounded.

"Sid's world…we brush up against it, but it's not our world," Ella explained. "It's a hard and ruthless world, and he's right to keep you away from it. To keep you safe. He loves you, India. What else could he do?"

There it was again. That word—the same one Sid had used to tell her what she needed to be, but wasn't—*ruthless*. It angered her. What did she have to do before he let her love him? Hit someone over the head with a bottle? Rob a bank?

"I want to tell you that you'll get over him in time," Ella continued. "But I don't think you'll listen to me."

At Ella's words, a deep truth, cold and stark and frightening, took root in India's heart. "I'll never get over him, Ella," she said bleakly. "Never."

"Well, then. What we can't get over, we must get used to," said Ella. "Goodness, did I just say that? I'm turning into my mother."

India gave her a small, sad smile. Then she gave her a hug, "Thank you," she said. With effort, she squared her shoulders and asked, "Who's next?"

"Fred Burke. Ten year old boy. Worms," Ella replied. "I think he—"

Ella's words were cut off by shouting.

"Please, Miss! Can you help us?"

India turned around. A girl was running toward her. She was holding a baby in her arms and clutching a small bundle in one hand. The baby's head lolled against her. His eyes were half-closed. His face was frighteningly pale.

"They said there's a doctor here," the girl cried. "Where is he? Can somebody please please help us!"

India sprang into action, alarmed by the sight of the suffering child, her own anguish instantly forgotten.

"I'm Dr. Jones and this is Sister Moskowitz. We'll help you. What's—"

Wrong, she was going to say. But the girl, crazed with fear, cut her off.

"He's my brother. His name's Alfie. Alfie Evans," she said, her words tumbling out. "He coughed up blood. It's consumption, he's got. That's what me mum had."

India held up her hands. "Calm down, Miss—"

"Ollie. Ollie Evans. Help him. *Please.*"

The girl was on the verge of tears now.

"I will. But you must help me, Ollie," India said, speaking slowly and soothingly to her. "You don't know what's wrong with him and neither do I, not until I examine him. Come this way..." She shepherded the girl toward the exam room. "Ella, I'll need—"

"—an aspirator, quinine, laudanum, camphor."

India and Ella were working as one, as they always did. Finishing each other's sentences. Thinking each other's thoughts. As Ella hurried across the yard to her house, and its kitchen, India rushed the two children past the other patients. Although everyone had been waiting patiently for his or her turn, no one protested. It was frighteningly obvious how sick Alfie Evans was.

India told Ollie to sit down on the examination table. Ollie did, placing her bundle down next to her. Just as she'd settled herself, the baby launched into a volley of coughing. India watched him, listening, her brow furrowing in concentration. She saw him lose his breath, struggle to regain it, then collapse against his sister.

Ella bustled back in with a basin of hot, soapy water and placed it on the examination table. As India washed her hands and dried them, Ella assembled implements and medicines.

"I'm going to listen to your lungs, little Alfie," India said, warming the end of her stethoscope in her hands before pressing it to the child's chest. Immediately she heard the high-pitched whistle of Alfie's breath passing over his swollen, congested airways.

India checked the baby's eyes and ears, then—over his weak, pitiful protests—got him to open his mouth, so she could look at his throat. She winced at what she saw.

"Is it bad, Miss?" Ollie asked, panic in her voice. "Is it—"

"It's not consumption," India said, pulling the stethoscope from her ears and hooking it around her neck.

"But the blood..." Ollie started to say.

"Alfie has bronchitis. And tonsillitis. His throat is so raw from the infection and the coughing that it's bleeding."

"Is bronchitis a bad one, Miss?"

"It's not a good one."

"Can you help him?"

The look of desperation on the girl's face was heartbreaking, but even so, India would not lie to her. Bronchitis wasn't tuberculosis, but it could still be a killer. Especially of children. "I will try my best," she said.

Ollie nodded vigorously, hope filling her tear-stained face. India saw that she was painfully thin. Her eyes were bright, but there were dark smudges under them, and hollows in her cheeks. She looked down at her brother.

"Why is he so quiet, Miss? He doesn't even cry anymore."

"Because he's exhausted and in pain and it's very hard to rally when you're tired and hurting."

Ella handed India a small aspirator, picked up the basin in which India had washed her hands, and hurried out of the exam room with it.

"I'm going to give him a few drops of a weak laudanum solution to relieve his pain and quinine to help fight the infection," India explained as she gently suctioned mucus from the baby's nose. "Then I'm going to rub camphor on his chest and put you both under a sheet with steaming water to open his lungs."

India had been refining her treatment for respiratory infections in children ever since Sid had brought a little girl named Jessie to her, suffering from whooping cough. She'd cured Jessie, and other children, and she desperately hoped she could cure Alfie, too.

When she finished with the baby's nose, she administered the medications. She wished the baby's mother were here. The woman was likely at work, but India needed to speak with her. The dosage would have to be repeated and laudanum was an opiate. Measuring out the right amount was a task she would only entrust to an adult.

"You said you were Alfie's sister…"

"Yes, Miss."

"Where are your parents?"

"Me dad's gone. He left us. Me mum's dead."

India's heart clenched. This girl had the care of a sickly child when she was barely more than a child herself. "I'm so sorry," she said.

Ollie looked away. "Alfie's all we've got left, me and my older brother, Jimmy. He means the world to us." She raised her eyes to India's and the worry in them deepened as she said, "I…I haven't got any money. But I do have something I can give you. Here…"

She nudged her bundle across the exam table.

"Ollie, that's not necessary," India said. "You don't have to give me anything."

"Yes, I do, Miss," Ollie countered, jutting her chin. "We aren't charity cases."

India didn't want to accept whatever was in the bundle; but she didn't argue. Life had taken so much from this girl. Pride was one of the few things she had left.

She unknotted the dish cloth that was wrapped around the bundle and gasped.

People brought her all sorts of things. She'd expected a couple of apples. Some carrots. Perhaps an old glass necklace or a hand-tatted doily.

She never expected a shiny brass faucet.

Chapter 12

"Is it not alright?" Ollie asked anxiously. "It's solid brass, Miss. It must be worth something."

India realized that her feelings were showing on her face and hastily pasted on a smile. "It's...it's perfectly fine," she said fumblingly, doing her best to recover from the shock of unwrapping her own stolen faucet. "Thank you. We can certainly use a faucet. And this is such a fine one."

Still smiling, she returned the stoppered bottles of quinine and laudanum to their shelf. Her mind was racing, trying to figure out how to get more information from the girl without scaring her.

"Where did you get the faucet?" she asked lightly.

"Me brother got it. Down the brewery. The foreman was getting rid of some fittings and he gave it to him."

"Did he now? How fortunate for your brother. And for me," India said.

She was certain the faucet was hers. It was brand new, made especially for hospitals with a high, curved spout, and marked with the manufacturer's stamp. Maybe the girl's brother had the rest of her stolen goods. Maybe she could get them back.

She took a glass jar down off the shelf, opened Alfie's grimy shirt, and rubbed a thick, greasy salve of her own devising on his chest, then she pressed a square of soft flannel over it. He protested a little, trying to bat the cloth away. India was pleased to see a bit of spirit in him.

Ella reappeared, a sheet over one shoulder, a basin of steaming water in her hands. She stopped dead when she saw the faucet sitting on the exam table.

"Crikey, where'd that come from? It's—" she started to say, but India cut her off.

"The perfect faucet for our new sink, isn't it, Sister Moskowitz?" she said, the fake smile still on her face.

Ella looked at her as if she'd lost her mind.

"Let's get young Alfie breathing a little easier, shall we?" India said, smiling harder.

Ella nodded. There were two battered wooden chairs in the exam room. India quickly turned them so they were facing each other, then Ella set the basin on one and Ollie on the other, with Alfie on her lap. India draped the sheet over them.

"There. We'll let the steam do its work now, Ollie. I'm going to step out of the exam room for a minute. I'll be back shortly to check on you," India said.

"All right, Miss," said Ollie, her voice muffled by the sheet.

India motioned to Ella to come with her. They hurried out of the shed—with India hastily apologizing to her patients again, reassuring them that she'd be right with them—and ducked behind it once more so they could talk without being overheard.

"Did the girl steal it?" Ella asked.

"I think her brother did."

"We need to get Sergeant O'Meara."

At that moment, Solomon walked by, heading toward the chicken coop with a bucket of potato peelings.

"Solly!" Ella hissed at him.

"What?" he shouted back.

"Shh!" Ella said, waving him over. "Run to the police

station! Find Sergeant Roddy O'Meara and bring him back here!"

"How much?"

"How much what?" Ella echoed, confused.

"How much will you pay me?"

"Solomon Moskowitz!" Ella scolded, glaring at him.

"Tuppence," India said, pulling a coin from her pocket and pressing it into his hand. "Go!"

Solly dropped his bucket and shot off.

"I hope he can find him," Ella said.

India hesitated for a moment, then said, "I do, too...I think."

"What do you mean, *think?*"

"That girl has no mother and a very ill baby to look after. She has enough trouble and I'm about to bring more down on her."

"Other people have troubles, too, India. Like the people we're building the clinic for. Those fittings cost the earth. And if Sid's right about the robbery, if Ollie's brother is somehow connected to Billy Madden, we'll need Sergeant O'Meara and his men to get the goods back."

"Yes, you're right, El," India said. "As always."

And then she returned to her patients. With Alfie and Ollie in the shed, she had to see the new cases wherever they were sitting—under the shed's awning, or somewhere else in the yard, with chickens scratching, cats roaming, and Miriam whacking the dirt out of a rug with a carpet beater.

The boy with worms. Another with impetigo. A girl with conjunctivitis. India got through them as efficiently as she could, dispensing medicine, applying salves, hushing howls, dodging flailing fists and feet. But there were more patients behind them. Always, always more. Each time she finished with a new one, she took a quick break to check on Alfie. She was encouraged to see that his breathing was easing, his eyes were open, and the pinched look was leaving his face. The steam and the medicines were working, but she knew that he and Ollie couldn't stay here forever. This was an old wooden shed, not a hospital. What would happen when they returned home?

India kept the two children under the sheet, refreshing the steaming water, for nearly an hour. She did her best to keep Ollie's spirits up, but her own heart was heavy. The girl had put her trust in India, and she had called the police on her. Olive Evans would never trust a doctor again.

"Where *is* he?" she whispered to Ella now, as she finished stitching a deep cut on a docker's arm. It felt as if an entire day had elapsed since they'd sent Solomon off and India was worried that the boy hadn't been able to find Sergeant O'Meara, but just as the words left her lips, they heard a voice from across the yard, near the kitchen door.

"Got him!"

Solomon was making his way down the back steps with the sergeant in tow.

"Indeed, he did," Roddy O'Meara said. "There are detectives I know who can't track a man like he can. He's got a future on the force."

Solomon crossed his arms over his chest. "How much are you paying?"

"*Genug!*" Ella hissed at her brother, shooing him away.

"The youngster said you need to see me. He said it was urgent," said Sergeant O'Meara.

India knotted the sutures she'd made and clipped the ends. "Ella, can you bandage Mr. Edmunds?" she asked.

Ella said she would, and India took the sergeant aside and told him about Ollie Evans and the faucet.

"Do you think she had a hand in the robbery, Dr. Jones?" he asked, when she had finished.

India shook her head. "She doesn't strike me as a thief, Sergeant. She strikes me as a desperate, worn-out child trying very hard to be an adult."

"I'd like to have a word with her."

India led the way to the examination room. Roddy O'Meara followed her. Once inside, his eyes darted to the faucet.

"Ollie, I have someone here who needs to speak with you," India said, as she folded the sheet covering the two children back.

Ollie looked at the helmet tucked under Roddy O'Meara's arm, at his uniform, his badge, and her arms tightened around her little brother.

"Please don't take him. Please don't take Alfie away," she said fearfully. "We're going to pay our back rent. Jimmy said he'd do it. Alfie won't last a day in the workhouse."

India removed the basin of water from the chair next to hers and put it on the floor. She sat down next to the girl. "Sergeant O'Meara is not here to take Alfie," she said gently. "He just needs to talk to you."

"About what?" Ollie asked warily.

"A few nights ago, a factory owned by Dr. Jones was broken into and some things were taken, including the brass faucet you brought here," Roddy O'Meara said. "I'm trying to find out who did it."

All the air went out of Ollie. She sagged back against the chair. "I knew it. I knew he was lying," she whispered. "Nothing goes right for us. Nothing ever goes right."

"Who, Ollie? Who was lying?" India asked.

"Jimmy. My brother."

"Tell us what happened," said Roddy O'Meara.

"We were hungry. And Alfie was coughing so," Ollie said, a tremble in her voice. "He's a good lad, our Jimmy. He never stole a thing until now. You have to believe me."

"How old is he?" the sergeant asked.

"Fourteen."

Roddy O'Meara inclined his head at that, as if he hadn't heard her correctly. "Did Jimmy have an accomplice?" he asked.

"A what?" Ollie said.

"Did he rob my building by himself?" India asked.

"I-I don't know."

"Do you still have my things, Ollie?"

"Some of them. Jimmy sold some."

India looked up at Roddy O'Meara. "I don't want to press charges," she said. "I would just like to have my goods back."

"Do you know where your brother took the goods? The name of the man he sold them to?" Roddy asked Ollie.

"He went to see Mr. Grizzard this morning," Ollie replied.

The sergeant bent his head to India's, talking low, so only she could hear him. "That's The Firm's favorite fence," he said. "If they didn't know who robbed you before today, they do now."

Ollie looked from the sergeant to India, her eyes wide. "Is Jimmy in trouble? You said you didn't want to press charges, Miss."

"I don't, Ollie. Please don't worry," India soothed.

"We just need to talk to your brother," Sergeant O'Meara said. "We need to find him..."

India finished the rest of his sentence in her head.

Before Sid Malone does.

⸙ Chapter 13 ⸙

It wasn't the stench that made tears well in India's eyes, a gut-tightening mixture of drains and dampness.

It wasn't the cracked plaster, the ragged quilt, or the mouse that ran over her foot as she stood in the center of the impossibly small room.

It was the piece of threadbare lace tacked up over the window.

It was a small thing and yet it spoke to India of a young girl's yearning for prettiness. Her hunger for privacy. Her small attempt at showing the world a bit of decency, even if it had shown her none.

India turned away from the window and set the things she'd brought from the clinic—medicines, a sheet, a milk bottle she'd filled with Mrs. Moskowitz's chicken soup—on a battered table, swiping at her eyes as she did.

Neither Roddy O'Meara nor Ollie Evans noticed. The sergeant was in the process of emptying a bulky flour sack out on the floor and Ollie was settling Alfie on the bed. India had accompanied them back to Ollie's room to help the girl continue Alfie's steam treatment. She'd left Ella at the clinic to finish seeing patients.

India stoked the embers in the fireplace now, added a few

lumps of coal, and set the tea kettle—filled from a pump located at the end of the street—over the grate. As she did, a cold, leaden weariness crept into her bones.

How will a sickly baby recover in this dreadful room? she wondered.

India pushed the feeling down, refusing to give into hopelessness. Alfie's best chance was Ollie, and she was determined to do everything she could to help the girl care for him. She'd briefly considered taking the baby to London Hospital but had dismissed the idea just as quickly. Since she had lost her position with Dr. Gifford, she no longer had privileges at the hospital and so could not treat the baby there. He and Ollie would be separated, which would distress him instead of keeping him calm and quiet, and there was no guarantee that the attending physician would follow her method of steam and chest plasters.

India found a battered tin pot, poured a few drops of camphor into it and put it on the table. As soon as the water boiled, Ollie could sit at the table with Alfie, the sheet draped over their heads, just as they'd done at the clinic. She had also written out the dosages for the laudanum and quinine on a piece of paper and had gone over them with Ollie. It was hardly ideal—a twelve-year-old girl dosing a baby with laudanum—but India could see that Ollie was capable, and she had learned that if she was going to wait for conditions to be ideal before she practiced medicine in Whitechapel, she was going to be waiting a very long time.

"Are these your things, Dr. Jones?" Roddy O'Meara asked, holding up a set of taps and a switch plate.

India recognized the goods. "Yes, they are," she replied, her heart sinking. She'd hoped that somehow it would all be a mistake, that Ollie would not be involved. "As I said before, I do not wish to press charges."

"Very well," O'Meara said, putting the goods back into

the sack. "I'll carry this back to your factory for you. It's on my way."

India thanked him and glanced at Ollie. She was still sitting on the bed next to Alfie, watching the sergeant, an expression of despair on her face. The only means she and her older brother had of feeding themselves, of buying medicine and coal, were being taken from them.

India reached into her pocket and pulled out two shillings. It was all she had on her. "Here, Ollie, take these," she said.

Ollie shook her head, her eyes downcast. "My dad said never accept charity, Miss. 'Robs your pride,' he said."

Heated words pushed at India's tongue. *And where is your father? Handing his wages over to some publican, no doubt. Posturing about pride while his children starve.* She bit them back.

"It's not charity," she said, kneeling down to the girl. "It's a helping hand. We all need one at times."

"You don't look as if you've ever needed help, Miss," Ollie said, unable to meet India's gaze.

"But I do, Ollie. More than you can possibly imagine," said India ruefully. She put the coins in the girl's hand and closed her fingers around them. "It's hard to accept kindness. It shouldn't be, but it is. It feels almost shameful. As if you're taking something that's not meant for you."

Ollie raised her eyes. "That's it exactly, Miss," she said.

"But here's the truth about kindness—it's not yours to keep," India told her. "You hold it close to your heart for a moment and then you pass it on. One day, Ollie, you'll pass it on, too. I know you will."

Ollie nodded. "Thank you," she whispered.

Roddy O'Meara picked up the sack of India's fixtures and slung it over his shoulder. He turned to Ollie. "Dr. Jones is good to drop the charges. Most wouldn't. But charges or no, I still want a word with your brother. When he comes back, tell him to find me at the station house. He's to come straight away."

"Is he still in trouble?"

"He will be if he doesn't come see me. Do you understand?" the sergeant asked, his tone stern.

Ollie nodded.

"Good," Roddy said. "Make *him* understand."

A moment later, he and India were walking down Thrawl Street.

"Is that nipper going to make it?" he asked.

"I hope so. He has a chance now. That's something."

The sergeant nodded, then went quiet.

"You're worried for the boy as well, aren't you?" India asked, reading the furrows in his brow, the grim set to his jaw.

"I am. The Firm aren't quite as forgiving as you are, Dr. Jones."

His words sent frost through India's veins. She remembered Sid's anger, his belief that a rival named Billy Madden was behind the burglary, and that Madden meant her harm. She remembered Sid's dire determination to find out who it was and punish him.

"Then we must find Jimmy Evans first, Sergeant," she said.

"Malone's men are already combing Whitechapel for him, I'm sure of it," Roddy said. "They usually know everything we know and then some. If I had to guess, I'd say they're paying someone in the station house for information."

Unlike the sergeant, India didn't have to guess if The Firm had an informant in the station house; she knew they did. *It's my business to know what happens in East London,* Sid had told her. Guilt needled at her conscience, urging her to confirm what Sergeant O'Meara suspected. But if she did, he would certainly want to know how she'd come by her information. And she could not tell him.

Come down off your high horse, India, Sid had once told her. *Step down into the mud with the rest of us.*

She'd taken his advice and then she'd learned that trudging through that mud was hard. It was easy to get stuck, to get lost, and there were times now when she dearly missed that high horse with its fine saddle. The ride atop its broad back had been so comfortable.

"Better yet, Dr. Jones, I'd like to find Sid Malone," the sergeant said, intruding on her thoughts. "He won't let himself be found, though. At least, not by me."

"I-I could try to see him," India ventured. "I do have…a sort of…I suppose you could call it access. As you know, he has contributed funds to my clinic. I could—"

Roddy O'Meara cut her off. "Please do not, Dr. Jones. It's going to be hard enough to find Jimmy Evans. I don't want to have to go looking for you, too."

"But Sergeant—"

"I'm happy to know that some of Malone's ill-gotten gains have gone to a good cause, but once a criminal, always a criminal."

"You do not believe in redemption?" India asked him.

"That's one for the man upstairs. Me, I believe the life Sid Malone has chosen ends one way—in the cold, hard ground."

His words were like a dagger made of ice, thrust straight into India's heart. She knew what she had to do. For Jimmy's sake. And Sid's.

They had arrived at her factory. The door was unlocked; George MacNeil and his men were there working. India and Roddy stepped inside, and Roddy put the sack down.

"Thank you, Sergeant."

"You're welcome, Dr. Jones. I'm going to try to find the lad. I'll go round to the landlord's. I know who he is," he said, as he took his leave. "If that fails, I'll wait for Jimmy at the flat. I'll be in touch. And Dr. Jones..."

"Yes?"

"Let me handle this. No visits to Sid Malone."

"Very well, Sergeant," India lied.

Roddy O'Meara set off up Gunthorpe Street. As soon as he was out of sight, India set off in the opposite direction. She started at a walk but soon broke into a run, panicked thoughts tumbling over one another in her brain. She needed to get back to her attic room at the Moskowitzes' to get money for a cab. She needed to get to Limehouse. She needed to find Sid.

Out on Wentworth Street, pedestrians clogged the sidewalks. Fording through them slowed India, so she veered into the street, stumbling a couple of times over the uneven cobbles. She had to tell Sid to call off his dogs, to tell him that the burglar was no rival, just a desperate, hungry boy. Sid would never hurt a boy; she knew that.

But Frankie Betts would.

India feared that Sid's violent, unpredictable henchman would kill Jimmy Evans without a second thought. Frankie would end Jimmy Evans' life, destroy Ollie's and Alfie's, and damn Sid forever. Sid yearned to leave the life; she knew he did. Roddy O'Meara was wrong; there was such a thing as redemption, even for Sid Malone. But not if Frankie found Jimmy Evans first.

As India neared the corner of Wentworth and Brick Lane, red-faced and sweating, she stopped dead and gave a cry of relief.

She didn't need to travel all the way to Limehouse. Straight ahead of her, standing in front of a tumbledown pub like an answered prayer, was Sid Malone's carriage.

Chapter 14

India hurried to the black carriage, panting for breath. She leaned against the door for a few seconds, trying to calm her pounding heart, her heaving lungs, then knocked on it.

From his perch at the front of the carriage, Ronnie craned his neck. When he saw her, he gave her a small, expressionless nod. She gave him an uncertain one in return, waiting for the door to open, but it did not.

Frustrated, she knocked on the door again. She tried to peer inside, but blinds were drawn over the windows.

Sid did not want to see her. He'd made that clear. But what he wanted didn't matter at the moment; she needed to see him. When he still didn't open the door, she banged her palm against it, mindful that she was drawing attention from passersby.

"Sid…*Sid!*" she hissed. "Open the door! I have to speak with you!"

The blind twitched slightly, but the door remained closed.

"Sid, please."

Finally, the latch clicked and the door swung open. It was so dark inside the carriage, India couldn't see Sid's face. She scrambled inside before he could change his mind, sat down, and reached back for the door handle.

"Sid, you must listen to me," she breathlessly began, the words rushing from her mouth. "You're wrong about the burglary at my factory." The door clicked shut. She sat back against the seat. "It wasn't—"

The words died on India's tongue, strangled by a sharp gasp.

The man sitting across from her wasn't Sid Malone.

He was thinner, and wiry, with the feral, merciless eyes of a wolf.

He was holding a knife in one hand, the butt resting against his thigh, the tip pointing up at her.

He was Frankie Betts.

Chapter 15

India's eyes darted to the door.

"I wouldn't," Frankie said.

In a slow, smooth motion, he leaned across the carriage and locked it. Then, still pointing his knife at India, he rapped on the wooden wall.

A panel slid open. "Where to?" Ronnie asked.

"No man's land," Frankie replied.

The panel closed with a short, sharp *snick*. Fear dragged a sharp talon down the back of India's neck, but she ignored it. Frankie Betts was trying to scare her. She refused to let him.

"Are you going to kill me, Mr. Betts?" she asked coolly, nodding at the knife. "If so, please go for the carotids. It'll be fast, though it will spoil Mr. Malone's carriage. But if you're not going to kill me, I have patients to see."

Frankie did not reply. He simply sat back in his seat, still holding the knife out, and regarded her. India felt the carriage pick up speed. They'd crossed Brick Lane by now, she reasoned, they must have, and were likely moving east on Old Montague Street, avoiding the traffic on the busy High Street. The talon at the back of her neck dug in deep.

"I don't have time for this, Mr. Betts," she said, forcing an impatient briskness into her voice. "What do you want?"

"I'd think something was going on between the two of you," Frankie said slowly, "but that's not bloody likely, is it? The guv likes his woman to look like a woman, all tits and ass. Not like a broomstick wearing spectacles."

India was not shocked by his ugly comment, or even surprised. She'd heard worse from male medical students.

"I hope your knife is sharper than your insults, Mr. Betts," she retorted. "Otherwise my death is certain to be a slow one."

The blow was so swift, so sudden, she never saw it coming.

There was a sharp crack. Stars exploded behind her eyes. Her head snapped back, hit the carriage wall, then lolled to one side. Her body felt heavy, as if it were filled with sand. She started to sag forward, certain she was going to collapse to the floor, but then the pain hit, white-hot and throbbing, dragging her back into consciousness.

Frankie had struck her with the flat of his hand, not his fist, but so forcefully that she could taste blood. It seeped from the corner of her mouth and dripped down her chin.

"Think you're clever, don't you?" he said. "Maybe now you'll watch what comes out of that smart mouth."

With shaking hands, India pulled a handkerchief from her skirt pocket and wiped the blood away.

Frankie was still holding the knife. He pointed the blade at her again. "If he's not fucking you, why did he give you money for your clinic?" he demanded.

"Because he is a friend to me and to the poor of Whitechapel and wishes to help them," India replied, struggling to keep her voice even.

"It's brought trouble on us. You've brought trouble on us."

India felt as if he hadn't heard her, as if he was talking to himself. She remembered what others called him, *Mad Frank*. Was he? She decided to try to reason with him.

"Is this about the robbery at my factory, Mr. Betts?" she asked. "Do you know who did it?"

"Of course I bloody know."

India's heart sank. She had feared as much. If Frankie knew, did other members of The Firm know, too? What if they were hunting for Jimmy Evans right now?

"If you know who did it, Mr. Betts, then you also know that he's just a boy, not part of a rival gang. He doesn't have designs on your turf."

"You don't know the first thing about us or our *turf*."

Frankie spat the last word, giving India a look of hatred so raw, she braced herself for another blow. When it didn't come, she gathered her courage and tried a different tack.

"Perhaps not, but I do know that you're not afraid of a fight, are you, Mr. Betts? A person's past is written on his body. And often his future, as well. A doctor can read so much of a patient's story simply by looking at him."

Frankie, dragging his thumb across the knife's edge, didn't answer her. India pressed on, hoping she could soften him. Make him sympathetic. Convince him to let her go and to leave Jimmy Evans alone.

"The crookedness at the bridge of your nose, for example...the thickness below the helix of your left ear...the dilation of your left pupil...they were all caused by taking some rather hard punches." She paused, searching for cracks in his sullen expression. "Were those blows meted out recently, or long ago? There's a slight bow to your legs, which tells me you had rickets as a child. And your right pinky...it scissors away from the ring finger. It was broken, wasn't it? But the bones were not reset properly. Or, perhaps, at all. Who broke it, Mr. Betts?"

She let the question hang in the air, her eyes on the knife, her nerves taut.

"You lived the same life that Jimmy Evans does," she said

softly. "A life of poverty, neglect, and abuse. You had no chance at anything better, did you? There was no one to give it to you. No one to help. Can't you be that someone for Jimmy Evans, Mr. Betts? Can't you be the one to give him a chance?"

The knife clattered to the floor. Frankie lunged at India and grabbed the cloth of her blouse with both hands. A cry escaped her as he yanked her forward.

"Shut yer fuckin' gob!" he shouted, his face only inches from hers, his eyes wild, lips flecked with spit. "You don't know nothing about me!"

He released her and she crumpled against the seat. Then he raised the blinds. Shaking, she followed his gaze and saw that they were traveling alongside the river now. The densely packed wharves and warehouses that lined the north bank were thinning out. She saw raddled scrubland and flashes of water—a dull, gunmetal gray under the brooding sky.

She saw something else, too.

That she was in a great deal of trouble.

No man's land, Frankie had replied, when Ronnie had asked him where he wanted to go.

A memory came to her now, of her history teacher explaining that the phrase came from the old English word *nonnesmanneslond,* the name of a forsaken area outside the walls of medieval London where executions took place.

There was a sudden sway as the carriage made a sharp right and turned off the main road onto a narrow, rutted one. And then India knew. And her fear turned into terror. He was taking her out to Rainham, a desolate marsh east of the city, miles away from anything or anybody.

There would be no one to see them out there. No one to hear them.

India had been so certain that Frankie only wanted to scare her, to take some sick pleasure from making her cry. But now, as she saw the marsh grass rippling in the breeze and the muddy tidal flats stretching out into the distance, she knew she was wrong.

She was going to die out here, begging for her life. There was no escape. Once the carriage stopped, it was over. If she tried to run back up the road, he would catch her. If she ran into the river, water would soak her skirts and drag her under.

"You can't do this," she said.

Frankie's eyes met hers. He gave her a soulless smile. "That's what people like you don't understand about people like me, Dr. Jones…I can."

☙ Chapter 16 ❧

"Where the hell is Frankie?"

Sid's question hung in the air unanswered until Desi, racking glasses behind the bar, turned and said, "You saw him leave this morning, Guv, same as me. He'll be back when he's back."

Sid had told Frankie to take his carriage so he could move around the city faster. That was hours ago. Ozzie and Tommy had left the pub on foot. Only Sid and Desi had stayed behind. The plan was for everyone to meet back here at the Barkentine. Why had no one returned yet? They'd been searching for the men who'd robbed India's factory since last night, but still hadn't found them. How long did it take to locate that git Delroy, or any of Madden's men? They were all as loud and as flashy as their guv, not the types to stay out of sight.

It was nearly noon now, and Sid, sitting at a table by the window, drained the mug of strong tea Des had made for him. Usually he'd have a pint in hand at this time of day, but he wanted to be at his sharpest when his men finally showed up, hopefully with a guest or two.

He was jumpy. Restless. His head ached. He dug his fingers into his temples, as if he could dig the pain out. Ever since last night, when Frankie had come to the Gaiety to tell him about the robbery, Sid had had to fight down the urge to pay a visit to Madden himself. He wished he could confront Billy directly instead of uselessly hanging about the Bark, but he was so angry that Billy had targeted India, he didn't trust himself to not beat the man silly, and get himself killed in the process.

Sid rose and walked to the bar now, barking at Des for another cup of tea, and as he did, the door to the pub opened. He spun around, ready for whomever, whatever, Frankie was about to drag inside, ready for a violent confrontation.

But he didn't get it.

"Hello, Mr. Malone," a female voice trilled.

"Hello, Gem," Sid said, standing up to greet her, and doing his best to mask his disappointment. Gemma Dean was the last person he wanted to see right now.

Stunning in a pink silk jacket and skirt, she walked over to him and kissed his cheek. She had to tilt her head to do it, to avoid catching him with the edge of her broad-brimmed hat.

"You left this in my dressing room," she said, handing him a flat wool cap.

"Ta, Gem. But you didn't have to come all the way over here to give it back to me."

"I was in the neighborhood," Gemma said. "Thought I'd drop by." She lowered her voice. "Truth is, I missed you. I thought we could go upstairs for a bit."

"It's not a good time," Sid said.

Her pretty face fell.

"I'm sorry, luv. It's business," he explained, his fingers working at his temple again.

"What kind of business?" Gemma demanded, pouting.

"Villains scrapping, what else?" Sid replied.

Gemma hesitated. She bit her lip, then gave him a feline smile. "Is it Billy Madden?"

Sid stopped rubbing his head. His sixth sense, the one he relied on the most, sharpened. "Why do you ask?"

"I wasn't going to tell you…"

"Tell me what?" he demanded, an edge to his voice.

But Gemma seemed not to mind his tone. In fact, her smile deepened.

"Madden booked a big suite at the Great Eastern last Sunday night. All week long, he begged me to come. But I said no. Then he said he had a gold ring for me with a ruby in it the size of a guinea. So I said maybe."

Sid took a step back, gobsmacked. He'd seen Billy Madden at the Great Eastern the night he was there with India, and was certain that Madden had been following him, trying to get something on him. Sid had worried that Madden had spotted India as well, and had put two and two together. Now he saw that he might be wrong. Madden had gone to the hotel with one goal—to get Gemma Dean into bed. He'd likely had no idea that Sid was there.

Gemma smiled at his speechlessness. "Why, Sid Malone," she purred. "I do believe you're jealous."

"Did you go?" Sid blurted.

Gemma looked as if he'd struck her. Her smile shattered. "Of course, I didn't go!" she said angrily. "I was only playing with him. Making a fool of him. Christ, Sid, what do you think I am?"

"I'm sorry, Gem," Sid hastily said, trying to backtrack. "I didn't mean it like that. I didn't think you'd sleep with the likes of Madden…I thought—"

"What? What did you think?"

Gemma waited, her arms crossed over her chest, for an answer. When Sid couldn't immediately come up with one, she answered for him.

"You hoped that I'd gone, didn't you? Because then I might have some dirt on Billy Madden for you. That's what you really want, isn't it? Seems he's the one you're hard for."

"Come on, Gem..."

Gemma backed away from him, shaking her head. Though she tried to mask it, Sid could see the hurt under the anger. She was a good actress, but not good enough to hide her heart.

"I told you about Billy because I wanted to make you feel possessive of me," she said. "But you're not."

"Of course, I am," Sid lied, hoping to placate her.

Gemma smiled again, but this time the smile was a sad one. "No, you can't be," she said. "A man only gets jealous over a girl if he loves her."

And then she turned and walked out of the pub, slamming the door behind herself.

It was perfectly quiet in the Bark for a long moment, then Desi broke the silence.

"Handled *that* like a champ."

Sid scowled at him. He felt terrible. He would send Gemma a ring twice the size of the one Billy Madden had dangled, and then he would end things between them. Gemma would find herself another villain, maybe it would be Billy. She was born and bred in East London and she knew how to survive it.

But India did not. And Sid realized now that his fear for her safety had compromised his judgment, leading him to see threats that weren't there and miss ones that were. He'd been so certain it was Madden who was behind the robbery of her factory, he'd barely considered other possibilities. But what if Billy wasn't behind it? While Frankie and the others were out trying to round up Madden's boys, the real perpetrators might still be out there, still circling. He'd tried so hard to keep India safe, but he saw now that he might have put her into even greater danger.

"You still want that second cup of tea?" Desi asked.

"I want a whiskey, Des. A double."

"Righto," Desi said, getting a bottle down off the shelf.

Sid walked to the bar, leaned his elbows on it, and rubbed

both of his temples now. The pain in his head was growing. His nerves were jangling. It was killing him to stay here, to stay put. Desi pushed a glass of amber liquid across the bar to him and he downed it in one gulp, grimacing as the whiskey burned his throat.

Sid motioned for another. While Desi poured it, the clock on the wall struck the hour—noon. As the last chime faded, Sid swore, then muttered the question he still couldn't answer.

"Where the bloody hell is Frankie?"

Chapter 17

India knew that she would never see Ella again.

Or her sister, Maud. Professor Fenwick, her mentor. Her parents.

She would never see Sid. Would he ever find out what had happened to her? It would destroy him to know that he was right—that she was not hard enough, not ruthless enough, to survive in his world.

The carriage came to a slow stop. Frankie unlocked the door and pushed it open. A breeze blew in off the river. India heard the marsh grass whisper and sigh.

"After you, Dr. Jones."

India shook her head. She flattened herself against the seatback. "I will not make it easy for you, Mr. Betts."

Quick as a cobra, Frankie struck. He grabbed India by her arms, yanked her off the seat, and threw her toward the doorway. She tried to stop her fall, to catch herself on the sides of the door, but couldn't and tumbled to the ground. Sharp stones at the road's edge bloodied her palms and bit into her knees through her skirt.

She raised her head and looked at Ronnie, high above her in his driver's seat.

"Help me, please," she said to his back, but he didn't so

much as turn his head.

"Get up," Frankie said, stepping out of the carriage.

When she didn't, he knotted his hand in her hair and yanked her to her feet. The pain was blinding; she screamed with the hot, electric shock of it.

Frankie forced her forward, through the marsh grass and the silty, sucking mud. Cold river water rushed into her boots, soaking her petticoat, dragging at her skirt.

"No...*no!*" she shouted, fighting him with all her strength. She twisted her body, trying to break his grip. She kicked at him. Her fingers scrabbled at his hands. But he was strong, and good at his work.

On he trudged, dragging India deeper into the river. When they were up to their thighs, he stopped and forced her to her knees. She gasped as the cold water swallowed her body, stopping just below her chin.

By some miracle, she had not lost her eyeglasses, and she looked helplessly up at the sky now, her heart slamming against her ribs, her breath coming in short bursts. How long before he pushed her head under? Before the filthy river water filled her mouth and nose?

"Bodies float, eventually. Did you know that?" Frankie asked her. "You've got to weight them or they bloat and pop up like a cork. You need a bit of rope. A nice flat rock or a chunk of iron. You've got to take your time and do it right. Long as you're thorough, no one ever finds them."

And then he released her with a vicious shove. Her head nearly went under, but she caught herself and lurched to her feet, frantically stumbling deeper out into the water to get away from him.

"This is your lucky day, Dr. Jones. I didn't bring any rope," he said.

He turned and started back toward the carriage and India

realized that he was going to leave her here.

"Don't hurt the boy!" she shouted after him.

"By the time you get back, it'll be over and done with," he shouted back, not bothering to turn around.

"You *can't*...for God's sake, he's just a *boy!*"

"He made his choices. Like we all do."

Frankie walked out of the river, stopping a few feet from the horses to stamp the mud off his boots, then he swung himself up into the carriage and closed the door. Ronnie turned the carriage around, cracked the whip, and the horses broke into a trot.

India watched as it pulled away and then grew smaller and smaller until it turned at a bend in the road and was gone. The instant it was out of sight, a convulsive fit of shaking gripped her. Anger pushed at the terror she still felt, and then both were washed away by a wild, giddy relief. Deep, gulping laughter shuddered up out of her throat but it quickly turned into sobbing. Tears streamed from her eyes. Her stomach heaved and she vomited. When the nausea subsided, she staggered out of the river and through the marsh grass, back to solid ground. And there, she collapsed, falling down hard on her backside, her body bruised and bloodied, her spirit crushed.

I've failed, she thought miserably, covering her eyes with her hands.

She would not be able to save Jimmy Evans. Frankie would kill him and without Jimmy to provide, Alfie would succumb to his illness. And what hope would there be for Ollie?

India didn't know what to do. She had no idea how she was going to get back to Whitechapel. She had no idea how she would face Ollie when she did, or Ella, or herself.

A group of gulls, screeching and brawling, pulled her from her thoughts. She lowered her hands and her eyes found them, wheeling around a ship coming upriver. Its hull was painted white. She squinted and saw that it flew a Spanish flag.

Oranges, she thought. *From Seville.* A patient, a docker, had told her that the fruit boats had white hulls to reflect the sun and keep their cargoes cool.

An image flashed into her mind. She saw Mrs. Barnett, her patient, handing the orange she'd given her to a child who needed it. She saw the old woman stop to lean on the door frame in the Moskowitzes' backyard, overcome by pain. Then she saw her knot her withered hand into a fist of defiance, and walk on.

And suddenly, she stopped crying.

Why am I sitting here? I've wasted so much time, she thought. Tears, regret, blame, despair—these things were useless. They got her nowhere. They didn't help Jimmy Evans. They didn't change anything for Ollie Evans. They didn't matter to Frankie Betts. An ocean of tears wouldn't have stopped him from killing her if he'd wanted to.

She saw that now.

And she saw something else that she had not seen before—that Mrs. Barnett was as hard as any villain, even harder. She might be racked by pain, but she refused to let it break her. She refused to let it take her selflessness, her kindness, her courage.

Mrs. Barnett did not sit on her backside crying.

"So why are you?" India said aloud.

Sprawled on the shore of the London river, with its dirty gray water lapping at her boots, and the sulfurous stench of its thick, clutching mud stinging her nose, India felt as if she'd undergone a baptism.

The river had washed her soul bare. It had revealed her to herself. And what she saw got her moving. She rose and started walking. Her clothing, wet and heavy, slowed her. Mud squelched from her boots. Her face throbbed where Frankie had hit her.

But she kept going.

Back to the road. To Limehouse, not Whitechapel. To the

Barkentine.

To save Jimmy Evans.

And God help Frankie Betts, or anyone else, who got in her way.

Chapter 18

A big pork pie. Six shiny red apples. Half a pound of chocolate biscuits with jam centers. Two bottles of medicine. And a painted wooden horse. One of its hooves was broken off, but Alfie wouldn't mind. All he'd ever had to play with was a rag with a knot for a head.

Jimmy Evans had been carrying these things in a bag for ages, trying to be careful with them. Trying to not bump the pork pie or bruise the apples or jostle the bottles. He was sick with worry. The medicines were for Alfie, but he hadn't been able to get back home to give them to him.

When he'd arrived at the landlord's house early that morning, he'd been told by the man's wife that her husband was out on business, but that he could wait if he liked. So he had. For over two hours. Finally, the landlord had showed up and Jimmy had paid off two months' back rent. The man had been surprised, but he'd gladly taken the money. Afterward, Jimmy had run to the chemist's and then the market. On his way home, he'd glimpsed the little horse in the dusty window of a junk shop and decided that Alfie should have it.

It was well past ten o'clock by the time he'd gotten back to Thrawl Street, breathless and sweaty. He'd been standing on the front step of his building, just about to go inside, when a hand had come down on his shoulder. He'd whirled around, arms tightening around his bag, ready for trouble. He'd expected Mel and his pack, trying to take his things from him. But it was only Eddie, a boy his age who lived one building over.

"Psst, Jimmy! Hey!" Eddie had said, pulling him down off the step and into a nearby alley.

Jimmy had angrily shaken him off. "What the hell are you playing at? And why are you whispering?"

"There's a copper in your room."

"*What?*"

"I seen him go in. He's got a woman with him."

Dread had clutched at Jimmy's heart. This was bad news. Ollie had taken the baby to a doctor, he just knew it. And now the police were here, no doubt asking where their parents were. He'd run a hand through his hair, his mind racing. What if the copper asked Ollie more questions? What if he frightened her into showing him the things Jimmy had hidden under the bed? If the police caught him, he'd go to prison. And then what would happen to Ollie and Alfie?

He'd felt the blood drain from his face at the thought.

"What'd you do, Jimmy?" Eddie had asked, giving him a close look.

"Nothin'," Jimmy had growled.

"All the same, I'd get out of here if I were you," Eddie had said.

Jimmy had nodded at his friend and then he'd bolted back up Thrawl Street toward the bustling Spitalfields market where he'd crawled into the back of a disused market wagon, under an old tarpaulin, and stayed hidden there for over an hour. Each minute had felt like a century, but the more time he let pass, the greater the chance the constable would tire of waiting for him.

Now it was past noon and he was back on Thrawl Street, about thirty yards from his house, eyes peeled for police. All he saw, though, were some kids playing, Mrs. Leary sweeping her step, a donkey cart, two barrows, and a black carriage. That gave him pause—you didn't see many carriages on Thrawl street—but then again, coppers didn't go 'round in carriages.

He walked down the street slowly, clutching his bag to his chest like a shield. Coppers were crafty and this one might still be around. He might be trying to trick him, to make him think he'd left when he hadn't.

Jimmy didn't hear the footsteps behind him until it was too late.

The pain felt like a bolt of lightning, searing and white, at the back of his head. He dropped his bag in the street. His vision blurred. His knees buckled. He pitched forward and the cobbles came at him, but a pair of hands grabbed the back of his jacket.

"Up you go, Jimmy Evans," a man said. His voice sounded watery and faraway.

Jimmy's guts tightened. It was the cop, had to be. One had been inside his house and one had been outside, watching and waiting. Ready with a cosh.

Jimmy tried to speak, to tell the man to leave off, he hadn't done anything, but his tongue felt thick and soft and all that came out of him was a groan.

He felt himself being hoisted to his feet, then half-carried, half-dragged to the black carriage. The driver opened the door. Jimmy was bundled inside and shoved onto the seat. He squeezed his eyes shut, trying to clear his vision. When he opened them again, he saw a man sitting across from him. He was wearing a jacket and trousers. No uniform, no badge.

Jimmy blinked at him, trying to get his head to stop spinning and his mouth to work.

Finally, the words came. "Who the hell are you?"

His question was met with a vicious backhand across his face.

Jimmy toppled over on the seat. His eyes fluttered closed. He was unconscious by the time the carriage's wheels rolled over his parcel, crushing the apples, smashing the biscuits.

Shattering the painted horse to splinters.

Chapter 19

The door to the Barkentine flew open and hit the wall with a crash, rattling the glass in its upper half.

"Get in there, you piece of shit!"

Sid Malone, sitting in a dark corner of the pub where he could observe without being observed, looked up in time to see a scrawny boy come flying through the doorway and land like a sack of rocks on the Bark's plank floor.

Frankie and Ronnie were right behind him. "On your feet!" he shouted, delivering a savage kick to the boy's ribs.

The boy tried to get up, but crumpled. And something inside Sid crumpled with him.

Is this what we've come to, the hard men of London? he wondered. *Getting children to do our dirty work? Acting like generals on a hill, sending boys to take the bullets?*

"Who's this?" Desi Shaw asked, walking out from behind the bar.

"The bleeder who robbed the factory on Gunthorpe Street," Frankie replied, breathing heavily from his exertions. "His name's Jimmy Evans."

Desi snorted laughter. "*Him?* You've got to be joking, Frankie. He's a bag of bones. He couldn't steal a lolly from a baby!"

"Oh, no? Ask Joey Griz. The little bastard went to him to

off a bag of brass faucets."

As Desi and Frankie were talking, the boy pulled himself up using the back of a chair, then stood there, dazed and swaying. Sid's eyes swept over him, taking in the blood on his head, his fat lip, the bruise coming up around his eye, all evidence of Frankie's handiwork.

Tommy and Ozzie, who had returned an hour ago, were playing cards at a table near the doorway. Ozzie turned around in his chair and gave the boy a onceover.

"How'd he do it?" he asked.

Sid wanted to know the same thing. "Lock the door," he said.

Frankie did so. Then he let the blinds down over the pub's windows, one by one. Jimmy Evans heard him do it; his hands, streaked with dirt and blood, tightened on the back of the chair.

Boy's hands, Sid thought.

"Give us a pint, Des," Frankie said, when he'd finished with the blinds. "I'm parched. Thirsty work, hunting this slippery blighter."

Ozzie continued to eye the boy up and down.

Jimmy Evans jutted his chin at him. "You a tailor? Sizing me up for a new suit?"

"No, yobbo, for a coffin," Ozzie said. "You know who you robbed?"

"Your great-aunt Fanny."

Desi, back behind the bar now pulling Frankie's pint, shook his head. "The flippin' cheek."

"You robbed *us,*" said Ozzie.

"How was I supposed to know it was your factory?" the boy asked. "Next time hang a sign on it."

Frankie slammed his hands down on the bar. He was back across the room in a few furious strides. "This is the East End, gobshite!" he shouted, cuffing the side of Jimmy's head.

"Everything belongs to us!"

Jimmy barely flinched.

He knows how to take a blow, Sid thought. *Wonder who taught him.*

"Nothing happens here without the guv getting a piece of it! My guv, your guv," Frankie continued, yelling into Jimmy's face. "East London's guv!"

Jimmy gave a sullen shrug. Frankie swore. He clenched his right hand into a fist, but before he could punch the boy, Sid stood.

"Not here, Frankie," he said, walking out of the shadows into the sickly yellow gaslight. "Too much blood. Take him in the back."

The boy's eyes flicked to Sid and widened, sending thin, snaking cracks through the mask of defiance he wore. Those who didn't know Sid by sight, knew him by stories. Sid said nothing to the boy, letting fear work upon him, letting it sink deep into his heart.

Frankie grabbed Jimmy and marched him into a room behind the bar. Sid followed and so did the others, eager to hear the answers to the questions he would ask.

There was a single light in the room and standing underneath it, a single chair. Frankie shoved Jimmy into it. Sid walked up to him, his steps slow and measured, until he was only a foot away from the boy. Then he stopped. He said nothing. He did nothing. He just gazed at Jimmy, his head slightly tilted, watching the cracks widen.

After a few long minutes, Jimmy finally broke. "You going to kill me?" he asked, his swagger gone. "I didn't mean—"

Sid held a finger to his lips. The boy fell silent.

"Now," Sid said. "There are only two things I want to hear from you, Jimmy Evans: how you robbed the factory…and who put you up to it."

Chapter 20

India's lungs were heaving; her heart was slamming.

The farm wagon, with two strong horses pulling it, had rolled along quickly from Rainham, but as soon as it entered London proper, the busy streets slowed it. It had crawled through intersections, stopped dead behind omnibuses, lumbered through Bow toward its destination—the Islington slaughterhouses, until a desperate India had jumped out and with a shouted *Thank you!* to the driver, had taken off running down the Burdett Road.

She was still running now. Faster than she ever had in her life, heedless of her aching legs and the painful stitch in her side. Past wharves and warehouses. Oblivious to the glances from furtive figures who skulked in doorways or peered from grimy windows. Every second that passed put Jimmy Evans deeper into danger.

Finally, she reached the edges of Limehouse. She thought she recognized the street she was on and followed its bend, certain that she'd emerge at Narrow Street where the Barkentine was, but the street dead-ended in a cluster of sooty, tumbledown houses.

"No!" she cried, turning in a confused circle, trying to think where she'd gone wrong. She'd traveled to the pub twice before, both times at night, but the riverside streets looked different in the daytime. They were noisy and bustling, clogged with traffic, disorienting.

She retraced her steps, hurrying back up the street and through an intersection. She saw a chandler's shop that she thought she remembered. Heartened, she started running again, found her turn, and made her way down the lonely, snaking street.

Over an hour ago, she'd stumbled out of the marshes and onto the main road. After she'd walked west for about two miles, she'd heard a wagon trundling behind her.

"Are you headed into London?" she'd shouted as it drew near. "I need a ride! It's an emergency!"

A man and woman were sitting in the driver's seat. They'd taken a look at her, muddied, bloodied and bedraggled, and then the man had hooked his thumb toward the back of the wagon. She'd ridden into the city hanging onto the wagon's high sides, trying not to skid in manure, bumped and butted the whole way by a dozen squealing pigs.

By the time she arrived at the Bark's front door, she was gasping for air. She leaned over, just for a moment, her hands on her knees, until she could draw a breath without wheezing, until her pounding heart stopped feeling as if it would burst. Then she grasped the doorknob and pushed. But the door didn't budge. It was locked.

She stepped back from the doorway and looked at the windows, dread plucking at her nerves. The blinds were all drawn, but light seeped out at their edges. How could the Bark be closed? Most city pubs opened early in the morning and stayed open until eleven o'clock at night. It was only three o'clock now.

She tried the door again, rattling the knob loudly. Surely someone was inside. Sid, some of his men, a bartender, someone who she could ask about Jimmy Evans. Someone who would understand that he was only a boy, one who'd made a terrible mistake.

And then, as she stood there, her hands on her hips, *she* understood. And her blood ran cold. Jimmy Evans himself was inside the pub. Frankie had found him and had brought him here. That's why the place was locked up tight, why the blinds were drawn.

India's mind swept her back to the horrible carriage ride she'd endured. She shuddered as she saw Frankie's face in her memory, contorted with rage, and terror unspooled inside her—not for herself this time, but for Jimmy. She threw herself at the door, battering it with her fists. She kicked it again and again. And when neither of those worked, she shouted.

"Frankie! Frankie Betts! Open this bloody door!"

She stood back, fists clenched, but still no one came. Betts had heard her—he must have—but he wasn't going to let her in.

India pressed her hands to the top of her head and paced. Trying not to give into despair. Trying to think. She remembered that the pub had a back entrance. It could be accessed when the tide was out.

Hoping against hope, she ran to the dank alley at the pub's east side and hurried down it, but when she came to the stone stairs that led down to the river's muddy shore, her hopes were dashed. The water was halfway up them.

With a despondent cry, India turned and started back up the alley. She had just reached the alley's mouth when she caught her toe and fell hard. Her eyeglasses flew off her face. Her knees, already bruised and torn, throbbed. Heedless of the pain, she felt for her glasses, found them, and put them back on. Then she got to her feet, turning to see what had tripped her.

A grim smile curved her lips as her eyes fell upon it.

There *was* a way into the pub. She had just found it.

Chapter 21

Frankie, his hand buried in Jimmy Evans' hair, pulled the boy's head back until all Jimmy could see was the ceiling.

"I say we cut the little bastard's tongue out. That'll teach him to tell lies."

"I'm not lying, I swear it," Jimmy rasped. "I done the whole job alone. Just like I told you."

Ozzie, standing at Sid's side, said, "Hard to believe, though, innit? Climbing up a building on a drainpipe? Then getting onto a skinny little ledge?"

Ronnie, standing on Sid's other side, said, "If it's true, the lad's got a lot of bottle."

Sid, leaning against a wall now, nodded. The lad certainly did have bottle. He'd told them how he'd robbed India's factory and he'd stuck to his story, despite Frankie's efforts to budge him from it. Frankie was mostly shouting, threatening, brandishing a fist. It was bark not bite, nothing more, not yet, but similar tactics had broken many a full-grown man.

"Who are you working for?" Frankie shouted now, leaning right down in the boy's face.

"Myself! *Myself.* I told you!"

Frankie let go of the boy, reached into his jacket, and pulled out his knife. "I just don't believe you, Jimmy," he said.

"A whole pack of villains couldn't have pulled that job off, never mind a kid."

Jimmy's eyes went round with fear. The blade, glinting in gaslight, shredded the last scraps of his bravado. He started to babble.

"I got the idea from a story I read. A long time ago. From a *Boy's Own*. It was about a geezer who did a job just like the one I done. But he robbed the Loover. In Paris. That's in France—"

"Aye, I know where bleedin' Paris is," Frankie growled.

Jimmy swallowed hard, then continued. "The man in the story…he stole a painting. An old one. He did his job alone and I did mine alone. Swear to God I did."

"Why?" Frankie shouted at him.

"For the dosh!" Jimmy shouted back. "Why else?"

Frankie gave Jimmy a shove. Then he walked over to Sid, leaned in close, and whispered, "I still think it's Madden. He'd send his granny up a downpipe if he thought there was two bob in it for him."

Sid didn't reply. His tongue felt as heavy as lead, but his heart was even heavier. There were six of them in the room with Jimmy Evans. Six grown men, terrorizing a teenage boy. How he hated them. How he hated himself.

Sid's silence scared Jimmy even more than Frankie's noise did. He started to babble again.

"I-I could work for you, Mr. Malone. I'm good at robbing," he said, his voice shaking. He nodded at the men in the room. "None of these could break into that building like I did."

The boy was right; they couldn't. Sid believed Jimmy. He believed the boy had acted alone. What he'd done was bold. It had taken guts and smarts. More than Billy Madden possessed.

He shouldn't be here with the likes of us, Sid thought. *He should be in school, learning things. A lad like that could do anything. The law. Or business. Discovering things. Inventing things.*

But East London didn't teach its boys what they could be, only what they couldn't. East London taught them how to do without. Without warm clothing. Without enough food. Without a chance, a prayer, a hope. Jimmy Evans was nothing but a boy, a boy already looking out at the world with the hard, weary eyes of a man. And Sid felt a rage rise inside him at the sheer fucking waste of it.

"I could break into shops, too," Jimmy continued, the words tumbling out of him. "I could—"

"Shut yer gob," Frankie said, scowling at him. Then he turned to Sid. "He disrespected you, Guv. He disrespected all of us." He cracked his knuckles loudly. "Will you do for him? Or will I?"

The question hung in the air.

Sid knew his answer spelled the end for Jimmy—not of his life, of his soul. There were some who could sanction the murder of a boy; but Sid Malone was not one of them. There was only one way to save Jimmy Evans' life, and save face for The Firm at the same time, and Sid saw it: he would make the boy one of them, just as Jimmy had asked. Then he would let it be known that he himself had set the lad to rob the building as a test, to see if he had what it took to join The Firm.

Jimmy Evans thought he wanted the life with its money and power. He didn't know, not yet, about the things that followed behind them like vultures—watchfulness, dread, and a constant, sharp-beaked fear that raked at your guts.

Well, he would find out soon enough. And then he would have to live with it, as they all did. Sid's decision was made. The words were on his lips, but he never got the chance to utter them.

Because at the exact instant he opened his mouth to speak, the frosted glass window in the Barkentine's front door exploded with an ear-splitting crash into a million jagged pieces.

~ Chapter 22 ~

"Guns. *Now,*" Sid said.

Frankie dove for the floor, fingers scrabbling at a plank. He wrenched it up, exposing a pile of loaded revolvers.

Hands grabbed for them, snatched them up, cocked their triggers.

"It's Madden's lads," Frankie said tersely.

"It's the law," Ronnie said. "Someone saw Frankie take the kid."

Whoever it was, Sid knew they'd come for him.

He looked at the boy. "Stay here," he told him. "If it's not our voices you hear when it's over, try to get upstairs and out a window."

Jimmy gave him a nod, then Sid and his men poured out of the back room into the bar.

And got the shock of their lives.

It wasn't a broken-nosed villain with a dozen of his best bruisers standing there before them.

It was a woman, slender and blonde, wearing spectacles. Her chest was heaving. Her fists were clenched. Behind her, the pub door, its frosted glass window now a jagged hole, stood ajar.

Sid's eyes kept telling him who it was, but his mind would not accept it. She looked like an avenging fury. Her hair, always neatly coiled at the back of her head, was hanging loose around her shoulders. Bits of what looked like grass were tangled in her curls. There was a bruise on her cheek, a smear of blood on her chin. Her once-white blouse was filthy. Her skirt was sodden, its hem caked with mud. A powerful stink was coming off her—a mixture of sweat, the stench of river mud, and something Sid couldn't place at first, then suddenly did...pig-shit.

He'd told her it was over between them. He'd told her to stay away. Instead, she'd thrown a brick through his window. He put his gun down on a table, hoping none of the men had seen that it was shaking in his hand. He could have shot her. Easily. Any of them could.

He wanted to shout at her. He wanted to tell her how furious he was at her for taking such an incredibly stupid risk with her life. But doing so would reveal to his men the very thing he had to keep hidden.

"What in God's name are you doing here?" he said, when he found his voice again.

India answered his question with one of her own. "Where is he?"

She waited for a response, but she didn't get one, so she bent down and picked up the brick she'd thrown.

"I (bang!)...said (bang!)...where (bang!)...is (bang!)... he (bang! bang! bang!)?" she shouted, slamming the brick on the table to emphasize each word.

"Have you lost your bloody mind?" Sid growled, his astonishment giving way to anger.

India ignored him. She looked around the room. Her eyes fastened on the light spilling from an open doorway in the narrow hall behind the bar.

She started toward it, but Frankie stepped in front of her, blocking her way.

"Just a minute—"

"Move," she said to him.

But Frankie didn't budge, and neither did India. They just stood and stared at each other, and Sid felt a raw, red fury moving between them, like a tremor along a fault line. They traded more words, but their voices had dropped low, too low for him to hear. And then, to Sid's astonishment, Frankie stepped aside. Something had passed between the two of them in that moment. A promise? A threat? Sid felt as if a truce had just been signed in a war he knew nothing about.

"Jimmy? Jimmy Evans?" India shouted, running down the hallway.

Sid's paralysis broke. "Oi! Where the hell do you think you're going?" he shouted, following her. The others were right behind him.

"Who are *you?*" he heard Jimmy say, as India entered the backroom.

"My name is Dr. India Selwyn Jones. I own the building you robbed."

"Are you going to hit me with that?"

India followed his gaze to the brick in her hand. She blinked at it, as if seeing it for the first time. Then, wincing, she dropped it. "Get up, Jimmy. You're coming with me."

Jimmy shook his head, regarding her warily. "I'm not."

Sid had entered the room now, too, with his men close behind him. They all saw her approach the boy. They saw her anger deepen as she took in the bloody cut on the back of his head, the damage to his face.

"No, of course you're not. Why would you?" she said. "God only knows what you've been through."

She turned and faced Sid. "You think he's working for a rival, don't you? Sergeant O'Meara told me that this is how the robbery would be perceived. I'm here to tell you that he is not."

Desi let out a long, derisive snort. "And how would you

know?"

"Because this morning, a twelve-year-old girl came into my clinic with a sickly baby—"

Jimmy was on his feet in a heartbeat, wild-eyed. "Was it Ollie? Was it her?" he shouted. "What's wrong with Alfie?"

India held up her hands, trying to calm him. "Alfie has medicine, Jimmy," she said. "He's being cared for."

She explained the baby's illness and what she'd prescribed to alleviate it, and Jimmy relaxed a little, but his hands stayed clenched.

"Thank you for fixing him, Missus," he said. He dropped his gaze to the floor. "I-I'm sorry I took your things."

"I accept your apology, Jimmy."

"I'll bring them back to you. What's left of 'em."

"Sergeant O'Meara has already done so," India said, then she turned back to Sid. "This boy lives with his siblings in a small basement room. It has one grimy window and is so damp that the plaster, what remains of it, is full of mildew. There are black beetles and mice. Their mother is dead. Their father provides nothing for them. They are all malnourished." As she spoke, her eyes found Sid's, then moved to every other man in the room. "You've never been in that room, but you know it all the same, every single one of you, because you come from rooms like that one, from families like that one. Jimmy Evans robbed me to buy food. *Food.* If I can forgive him, surely you can?"

You bloody woman, Sid thought. *You brave, stupid, shit-splattered fool.*

The men in the room with him...each one of them could take a blow. They'd had fists aimed at their faces, coshes aimed at their skulls. They had teeth knocked out, ribs cracked, arms broken. It was part of the job and if his men knew anything, it was how to throw pain off. Wounds closed. Bones healed. No hard feelings. Forgive and forget.

But India had aimed at their hearts; and that was a blow they could never forgive.

There was only one way out of this now, and Sid knew he had to take it. "It doesn't change the fact that Jimmy Evans did what he did on my turf," he said to her. "And that was a mistake."

India's eyes widened at his words; she opened her mouth to protest, but Jimmy spoke first.

"Can you give these to my sister, Missus?" he said miserably, pulling a few coins out of his pocket. "Can you…can you tell her I tried me best?"

"Give them to her yourself, lad," Sid said.

Jimmy's thin body slumped with relief at Sid's reprieve. A weary smile lifted the corners of his mouth. "Thank you, Mr. Malone. You won't regret it. I'll work hard for you, I swear."

But Sid had come up with another idea. "Oh, you'll work hard all right, lad. But not for me," he said, shifting his gaze from Jimmy to India.

India met his gaze, the anger in her eyes giving way to confusion.

Sid's men were bewildered, too. They were all adept at silently deciphering the meaning of his words, but now they traded baffled glances, unable to crack the code.

Then Frankie finally twigged, and ugly, raucous laughter burst out of him. "You poor fucking bastard," he said to Jimmy.

One by one, the rest of the men figured it out, too.

"You can't be serious, Guv," said Ozzie.

Ronnie shook his head. "That's vicious, that is."

"Changing some crusty toe rag's bandage," said Frankie, still laughing. "Cutting some tosser's arm off. Looking down one end of a bloke and up the other. Cleaning up blood and sick and pus and—"

"Blimey, Frankie, leave off," Desi said queasily.

"I-I don't understand," said Jimmy, looking from Sid to Frankie and back again.

Sid hooked a thumb in the direction of the loo. "Go wash your face, lad."

Jimmy took a hesitant step forward then stopped, his uncertainty deepening.

"You heard the guv. Clean yourself up," Frankie said. "You're taking a ride."

"Where to?" the boy asked.

"Brick Lane," Frankie replied. He put an arm around Jimmy and patted his cheek. "Turns out we're not going to kill you, you tosspot. You'll only wish we had."

"You're working for Dr. Jones," Sid said.

"What?" India cried. "No, he's bloody well not!"

"No, I'm bloody well not!" Jimmy yelped.

Sid pinned the boy with his gaze. "Hear me, lad," he said. "This is the first, last, and only chance I will give you. Do you understand?"

Jimmy closed his mouth; he nodded.

"This is absurd!" India protested. "You don't really expect me—"

Sid cut her off. "You wanted to rescue him, didn't you? So now he's rescued. And now he's yours."

He was gratified to see her take a step back, flustered.

"But...but what am I supposed to do with him?" she asked.

"That's your problem, Dr. Jones," said Sid. He turned to Ronnie. "See that the doctor and her charge get back to Brick Lane." And then he left the room.

"Mr. Malone? Mr. Malone, wait!" India called after him.

But Sid was already gone. Out of the pub. Out of her reach. He would unravel in front of his men if he stayed in the Bark one second longer. From fury. From fear. From awe.

Jimmy Evans's life was worth so little. Children like him were two-a-farthing to most of the world, but not to her. Six desperate men, men who'd thought they might be about to lose their own lives, had pulled guns on her. One mistake, one jumpy trigger finger, and he would have had to watch her die on a dirty pub floor. *Her.* The woman he loved beyond all reason.

All to save a ragged boy.

And so he walked away, hard and fast, rather than stay and face the truth.

That India had come to the Bark not to save one life.

But two.

❧ Chapter 23 ❧

India stared into her empty bowl. She'd eaten the chicken soup so quickly, she'd burned her tongue. The hot broth, with flecks of parsley and circles of fat shimmering on its surface, had brought some life back into her weary, aching body.

"This soup could probably cure more people of more ailments than all the doctors in London," she said.

"There is no probably about it," said Mrs. Moskowitz, ladling another helping into her bowl.

India thanked her. She needed the second helping; she was reeling. From her carriage ride with Frankie Betts. From seeing half-a-dozen loaded guns pointed at her. From Sid handing her the responsibility for a fourteen-year-old boy. And then walking away. Again.

She looked at Jimmy Evans, sitting at her left, elbows on the table, head down, greedily slurping his soup, and dismay clutched at her heart.

What on earth was she going to do with him? He was a problem she had no idea how to solve.

It was just after six o'clock now. India had arrived at the Moskowitzes' with Jimmy in tow an hour ago. He'd wanted to go straight home, but she'd insisted that he come with her first so she could tend to the injuries Frankie Betts had inflicted on him. After that, they would go to Jimmy's flat together so she could check on Alfie.

The backyard clinic was closed when they arrived, the patients gone, but Ella was still there, cleaning up after a busy day. Her eyes had gone as round as two pie plates at the sight of them.

"Bloody hell, India, what happened to you? And who is this?"

"It's a long story," India had said.

"Tell it at supper, then," Ella had said. "Go wash. And change your clothes. You look terrible and you smell even worse." She looked at Jimmy. "I'll take care of him. He can eat something, too. What's your name, lad?"

The boy, his eyes on the floor, hadn't answered. So India had.

"Jimmy Evans."

Ella's jaw had dropped. "Ollie's brother?"

"Yes."

"I'm guessing that long story of yours will also be an interesting one," Ella had said, shaking her head.

A few minutes later, India was standing naked in a large enamel basin, in the small, curtained scullery off the kitchen, pouring water from a large pitcher of water over her head, thankful that Mrs. Moskowitz was busy in the café counting the day's earnings and hadn't seen her come in. There would be explaining to do, but she wanted to clean herself up first.

She'd worked soap through her tangled hair with her fingers and scrubbed her body with a washcloth. Then she'd rinsed the mud and blood off, wishing she could rinse the day's awful memories off, too.

She'd thought that nothing could scare her more than her trip to the river with Frankie, but she was wrong. Standing face-to-face with him in the Bark, knowing she had to get past him to save Jimmy, was every bit as terrifying.

At first, Frankie had told her he would not let her pass.

"You will, Mr. Betts, or I shall tell Mr. Malone what you did."

"Go ahead, Dr. Jones," Frankie had said. "He won't care."

"I think he will. You assaulted a woman, one who happens to be his friend. I don't know Mr. Malone very well, Mr. Betts," India had lied, "but I do not believe he approves of battering women. And I think he'll assault *you,* and perhaps Ronnie, too, if he finds out. Perhaps he will even throw you both out of his gang. Shall we find out?"

Frankie Betts loved Sid; India saw that. He had no life other than the one Sid had given him. She had bet on that love, meeting Frankie's cold, soulless eyes, not looking away from the darkness behind them, forcing him to choose: Jimmy or Sid.

And he had chosen Sid. He'd stood aside and allowed her to go to Jimmy, and she had kept their secret. She would continue to keep it. She despised Frankie Betts, but a deal was a deal.

After scrubbing herself, India had toweled her body dry, then put on the fresh clothing she'd grabbed from her room and a pair of slippers. She would clean her boots later. Then she'd dumped the dirty water down the drain in the center of the floor, rinsed the basin in the scullery sink, and hurried to help Mrs. Moskowitz and Miriam with the supper preparations. She'd entered the kitchen at the same time Ella had.

Mrs. Moskowitz—who'd finished counting the day's earnings and had turned her attention to a large pot of soup simmering on the stovetop—had taken a startled look at India's bruised face, and then at the thin, ragged boy with Ella who would not raise his eyes from the floor.

"Miriam," she'd said, "set an extra place at the table, please. And fetch a bottle of wine. I think we will need it."

They'd been joined in short order by Yanki, returning from

shul; Aaron, coming back from a late-day market run; Solomon and Posy, feathers in their hair from plucking chickens in the yard; and Mr. Moskowitz, back from the corner newsstand with the evening paper under his arm.

"Who's he?" Solomon had asked, hooking his thumb in Jimmy's direction.

"The cat's brother," Ella had replied. "Mind your business and put the bread on the table."

"Why's he so skinny? Why does he have a cut on his head? Is he staying for supper? Where does he live?" Posy had asked.

"Wash your hands. It's suppertime, not twenty questions," Mrs. Moskowitz had chided.

Glances had been traded among the Moskowitz children. One-by-one, they'd taken their seats around the table. Soup had been served. Thick slices from a large loaf of fresh rye bread had been passed, along with a dish of salted shmaltz to spread on them.

When wine had been poured for the adults, and all had food in front of them, Mr. Moskowitz recited the blessing. As soon as the last words left his lips, Mrs. Moskowitz had asked India what had happened, and everyone around the table had listened intently to her answer. She'd told most of the story, including Jimmy's part in it, and the showdown at the Bark, but she'd left out her trip to Rainham, blaming her cuts and bruises on a fall. She'd also left out the guns; the Moskowitzes had been shocked enough by what she did tell them. She'd glanced at Mrs. Moskowitz a few times as she was speaking, and Mrs. Moskowitz's expression had told India that she did not believe she was getting the entire truth, but to India's relief, she had not pressed her for it.

"I don't want to work for the doctor," Jimmy Evans said now, his eyes glued to his soup bowl. "I don't like blood. Or sick. Or coughs."

Mrs. Moskowitz frowned at him. Then she banged her palm on the table to make him look up. "Listen to me, Jimmy Evans," she said. "No one likes these things; that is beside the point. You do not have a choice. You must do as Mr. Malone has said. He is not a man to be trifled with."

Jimmy nodded. He dropped his gaze again. "Yes, Missus," he said quietly.

"You will work for the doctor," Mrs. Moskowitz continued. "Five days a week and a half-day Saturday. She will pay you." She looked at her husband. "What amount do you think is proper, Mr. Moskowitz? Two pence an hour? For a nine hour day that would come to one shilling and sixpence."

Mr. Moskowitz took a bite of bread and chewed it, his brow furrowing in thought. Before he could offer his opinion, Mrs. Moskowitz continued.

"Then again, one must take into consideration that Jimmy Evans is clearly a bright boy, and an enterprising one, too. Imagine climbing up so high off the ground for a few faucets! Many others would like to hire a boy with such *chutzpah,* I am sure." She paused for a moment, still looking at her husband, then said, "Yes, Mr. Moskowitz, you are right once again...one shilling and sixpence is not enough. Two shillings a day. That is the correct amount to pay this boy." She turned to India. "You can take his wages from the money Mr. Malone gave you."

"Looks like that's settled," Ella observed wryly.

"It certainly does," India agreed.

She'd thought that Jimmy Evans was a problem that was hers to solve, but she should've known that Mrs. Moskowitz would never let her carry such a burden alone. What concerned one Moskowitz concerned the whole family, and India was one of the family now. As she looked at them all—talking, eating, arguing, laughing—her chest felt too small for her heart.

With the decision made, Mrs. Moskowitz looked to see

whose soup bowl was empty. Jimmy's was. She ladled another helping into it.

"How much more is he going to eat? He's already had two bowls!" said Solomon in an aggrieved voice.

"Solly!" Ella scolded. "That's rude!"

"Are you an accountant now, Solomon Moskowitz?" Mrs. Moskowitz asked her son, arching an eyebrow. "I am very glad to hear it. Half the plum cake I baked this morning is gone. Perhaps you can account for that."

Solomon flushed red.

"Solly! You ate half the plum cake?" Posy echoed, outraged. "Mama, that's not fair! He ate up the babka the other day, too. He shouldn't get any pudding for a week!"

"An accountant *and* a lawyer," Mrs. Moskowitz said. "I shall be well provided for in my old age."

Jimmy Evans shyly raised his eyes to Mrs. Moskowitz's. "Thank you for the soup, Missus," he said.

Mrs. Moskowitz smiled at him. "I am glad you liked it."

"It was very good. My mum cooked like that. A long time ago. Before things got bad. Before...before she died," Jimmy said, dropping his gaze again.

The conversation fell away. Everyone looked at Jimmy, saddened by his admission.

Posy was the first to speak. "You don't have a mum?" she asked.

Jimmy's grip on his spoon tightened. He shook his head.

"I'll share my mum with you, if you want," Posy offered. "She's a good mum. My dad, too. He's a nice dad. He doesn't talk as much as my mum, though."

"No one does," said Aaron.

All the Moskowitz children laughed out loud at that. Mr. Moskowitz cracked a smile. Mrs. Moskowitz swatted Aaron and tried to look offended, but even she couldn't help but laugh.

Aaron, still grinning, asked Jimmy to pass the bread, then he asked him who his favorite boxer was. The two boys fell into a spirited debate over who had a better right hook—Ted Pritchard or Jem Smith—and India guessed it had been a long time since Jimmy Evans had enjoyed not just the warmth of a good soup, but the warmth of companionship and laughter, too.

"Clear the table, please," Mrs. Moskowitz said when everyone had finished eating. "And bring what is left of the plum cake."

The younger children rose and took away the dirty dishes. Jimmy helped them. Then they brought the cake. Yanki said he didn't want any and went upstairs to study. Ella rose to fetch some patient records that she wanted to review. Mr. Moskowitz left to read the evening paper in peace and quiet.

As the children ate their dessert and chattered amongst themselves, India finished her glass of wine, waiting for Jimmy to finish his cake so she could walk him home. She was still worried about the boy and his siblings, and still shaken by the day's events. She knew she would have to find Roddy O'Meara tomorrow morning, who had also been looking for Jimmy, give him the same version of the story she'd given to Mrs. Moskowitz, and hope he wouldn't ask too many questions.

"You are still troubled, my darling India," Mrs. Moskowitz said to her.

India nodded, realizing that her feelings were showing. "The clinic, my patients, the factory renovations, and now this boy," she said quietly, glancing at Jimmy. "I can give him a job. I can try to train him. But he needs more. He needs his parents. A new flat. His sister should be in school, not looking after the baby. Jimmy Evans needs so much more than I can give."

Mrs. Moskowitz's warm eyes filled with understanding. "Did you go to church as a child?" she asked.

India tilted her head, perplexed by the strange question.

"Yes, I did."

"Then you know it is very difficult."

"What is difficult, Mrs. Moskowitz?"

"Saving people. Even your messiah had a very hard time of it. He suffered terribly. And he could have avoided it. He could have told the Romans what they wanted to hear. He could have run away, but he did not. I have often wondered why." She smiled ruefully. "We try, my darling India, but even the best of us fall short. We shout at the neighbor. Snap at our children. Kick the dog. And far worse. If Jesus saw these things and still decided to trouble himself on humanity's behalf, perhaps you can, too."

"Are we still talking about Jimmy Evans?"

Mrs. Moskowitz patted India's hand. "Of course, *zeeskyte.* Who else?" she said, rising from her chair. "You must take some soup to the boy's sister and brother."

India watched her go. Once again, Mrs. Moskowitz had understood all the things she had said, and all the things she had not.

Ella, back with a stack of patients' records in her hands, sat down again at the table next to her.

"She knows, doesn't she?" India said. "About Sid and me."

Ella glanced at her mother, ladling soup into a jar. "Of course she knows. She knows everything. I have no idea how." She paused for a moment, her eyes traveling over India's mottled cheek, her swollen lip. Worry creased her forehead. "Unlike my mother, I don't know everything," she continued. "But I do know this: You didn't get those marks on your face by falling down."

India felt the blood rising in her cheeks at Ella's words. She looked away.

"Let him go, Indy," Ella urged. "I've told you before... you're not meant to mix in his world. You want to save someone?

Save Jimmy. Save Ollie and Alfie." She covered India's hand with her own, squeezing it hard. "Save *yourself.*"

Chapter 24

"Hold still, Martin, you little bollocks!" Jimmy shouted.

"Don't call my boy a bollocks!" Mrs. Meecher shrilled.

"Six years old and still sticking things up his nose? If that ain't a bollocks, Missus, I don't know what is!"

"Jimmy..." India cautioned, between gritted teeth. She was inside her small exam room with three other people trying to see into a wriggling boy's inflamed nostril.

"Mum, save me!" Martin howled, trying to sit up.

"Listen you, I said hold still!" Jimmy scolded, tightening his grip on the boy. "Or the doctor will miss and poke a hole in your head! You know what happens then? All the air leaks out, just like a popped tire!"

Martin stopped squirming. He stopped shouting. He lay as still as a statue on the examination table, saucer-eyed. And an instant later, India pulled a small hard object out of his nostril, pinched between the prongs of her tweezers.

"There we go," she said, turning the object this way and that. "What is it, I wonder? A bean?"

"His brain," Jimmy said flatly.

After a handful of lemon drops hastily offered by India, and an apology grudgingly offered by Jimmy, Martin and his mother left. As soon as they were gone, India upbraided her new hire.

"Jimmy, your behavior with Martin was atrocious."

"It worked, didn't it?" Jimmy said. "The little git held still."

"That is not the point," India retorted. "My patients expect me to be compassionate and honest; they do not expect me to call them names and tell them frightful, made-up stories."

"I *was* honest, Dr. Jones. Martin *is* a bollocks," Jimmy protested. "He's in here every week with something stuffed up somewhere. Ask me, that lad is a few cards short of a full deck."

India closed her eyes. She pinched the bridge of her nose, pushing her spectacles up to her forehead. "What did we talk about yesterday? What have we been talking about ever since you started here?"

Jimmy sucked in a noisy, put-upon breath, then blew it out. "Not making faces in front of the patients. Not holding my nose in front of the patients. Not gagging in front of the patients..."

"And?"

"Not mouthing off at the patients."

"Which is all part of?"

"Bedside manner."

"Correct. Now please endeavor to show some," India said. She readjusted her glasses and opened her eyes. "See the next patient in."

As India wrote up her notes on Martin, Jimmy fetched her next case—a middle-aged woman with a stomach ailment.

"You're too flippin' skinny, Mrs. Gallagher, that's your problem!" India heard him say, as he led her into the exam room. "How d'you expect to have any vitality if you don't eat?"

India did something then that she rarely did; she swore. Under her breath. Jimmy Evans was driving her mad. He'd been working at the clinic for two weeks now, had been lectured dozens of times by herself and by Ella, and still couldn't manage to behave himself.

"Good afternoon, Mrs. Gallagher," she said to the woman. "Have a seat. I shall be right with you."

Then she turned to Jimmy. "Come this way, please," she said sternly, taking him by his elbow and leading him out of the shed, through the waiting area, and into the yard.

"Mrs. Gallagher does not choose to be thin," she said when they were out of earshot of any patients. "She suffers from severe gastric reflux which makes eating difficult for her. It is not your place to diagnose or advise patients. You are to do exactly as I tell you. No more and no less. Do you understand me?"

"Yes, Dr. Jones," Jimmy said contritely.

"Good. Now go fetch me some clean basins from the kitchen."

India watched him go, her hands on her hips.

When he was halfway to the kitchen, he turned back to her and said, "The sphincter, right? The one between the esophatus and the stomach. It doesn't tighten all the way, which means stomach acid comes up and damages the esophatus, which can make for ulcers. And cancer."

India softened a little. "Esopha*gus*. But very good," she said. The boy had clearly listened yesterday when she had examined a man with the same complaint.

Jimmy grinned. He gave her a cheeky salute and disappeared into the Moskowitzes' kitchen. India rolled her eyes, then went to attend to Mrs. Gallagher. After she finished with her, Ella bustled in with a tall stack of folders for the next group of patients.

"How's our boy today?" she asked.

"Irksome, as usual," India replied, scribbling her notes on Mrs. Gallagher. "He called one patient a bollocks. And presumed to diagnose another."

"You don't know the half of it," Ella said. "This morning, he told Mrs. Nesbitt that her newborn looks like Queen Victoria, and called the little boy who came in with the bad rash *Polka-dot Pete.*"

"I've warned him. I've told him we'll have to let him go if he doesn't mind his manners," India said, sighing. "I can't have him insulting our patients."

"I don't know why he does it. It's as if he can't help himself."

India put her pen down. She looked at her friend. "I think it's because he's bored, Ella," she said.

"Bored?" Ella scoffed. "He can't be. We run him off his feet."

"Yes, but we have him fetching supplies, emptying rubbish bins, sweeping floors, washing basins..."

"What's wrong with that? It's good, honest work and he's glad to have it. He told me so."

"Last week, I loaned him one of my old anatomy textbooks," India said. "The next morning he recited every muscle, bone, blood vessel, ligament, and tendon in the foot."

Ella nodded, as if India's words had confirmed her own thoughts. "He already knows the symptoms for most of what we see—catarrh, neuralgia, rheumatism, lumbago, pleurisy..."

"He's memorized the treatments and prescriptions for them as well."

"You saved a bright lad, India. That's a good thing. So why do you look so troubled?"

India cast about for an answer. Jimmy could be very trying but she was pleased with his eagerness to learn. At the end of every day, however, when he finished his work, said good-bye, and started for home, she felt heavy-hearted. The desperate, hopeless feeling she'd confessed to Mrs. Moskowitz right after Sid had lumbered her with the boy had only grown.

"Maybe I did save him," she said at length. "But for what? When I was his age, my family's wealth afforded me an education. Jimmy Evans has no such option. What am I doing besides making a poor boy hungry for a world he will never enter?"

"What are you doing?" Ella echoed, incredulous. "Quite a lot. Jimmy earns a decent wage now. His family has a warm room and enough to eat. Alfie has recovered."

"But it's not enough, El. Jimmy Evans is smart. Maybe even brilliant. He's meant for better things."

"Oh, Indy," Ella said, shaking her head. "You still want to save the world, don't you? Whitechapel hasn't knocked that out of you yet." She put the folders she was holding down on the table. "Why don't you start with your next patient...Mr. Timson? His piles are acting up again. And don't forget that you have house visits tonight. I can't go with you. I have to sit shiva with my mother. Her friend's husband died. Take Jimmy."

India groaned.

Ella feigned a look of concern. "What's wrong, Dr. Jones? Are you not well?" She made a show of feeling India's forehead. "Hmm, in my professional opinion, you and Mr. Timson are suffering from the very same affliction."

India gave Ella a look. "We certainly are *not*."

"Oh, but you are," Ella said, with a teasing grin. "You both have a giant pain in the arse. Mr. Timson has his piles, and you have Jimmy Evans."

Chapter 25

Sid Malone, leaning one hip into the bar, lifted a glass of porter to his lips and took a deep swallow.

He was thirsty. It was dark, nearly nine o'clock now. He'd just entered the pub after walking the narrow streets around the St. Katharine's docks. A load of paintings had arrived on a ship from France and were being warehoused there. Rumor had it there were two Vermeers among them, a Holbein, and a Rembrandt. Griz had a keen buyer; all Sid had to do was get the goods. He'd cased the docks until the night's drizzle had turned to a proper rain. It would be a difficult job to pull off, but Sid relished the challenge. It gave him a goal. Focused his thoughts. It took his mind off India.

He missed her, every minute of every day. He wanted to talk with her, touch her, make love to her…and tell her off.

He was angry at her, still. A fortnight had passed since she'd thrown a brick through his window, and he had no idea how she'd found out that Frankie had snatched Jimmy Evans. It was possible, he reasoned, that she could've seen Frankie do it. From what she'd said in the Bark, it seemed she'd been to the boy's flat, and she would have known where Frankie was likely to take him. But none of that explained why she'd been so dirty and disheveled. Sid wished he knew the answers to these questions. Most of all, he wished he knew what had passed between India and Frankie when Frankie had tried to stop her from getting to Jimmy.

He'd asked Frankie about it, but Frankie had merely shrugged and said, "Don't know what you mean, Guv. I was just giving her evil looks, trying to scare her into leaving without putting my hands on her. I'd never rough up a woman."

It was a perfectly reasonable answer, but for some reason Sid didn't buy it. He wished he could ask India the same question, but that wasn't going to happen, not after he'd told her he wasn't going to see her anymore.

He'd been wrong about the reason for his decision—Billy Madden wasn't the one who'd robbed her factory. But still, he'd done the right thing in ending it with her; he was certain of that. If it wasn't Madden looking to get at him through her, it would be someone else.

Sid's glass was almost empty. He drained it and was about to motion for another, when the pub door opened, and he nearly dropped the glass on the floor.

It was her. She was here. In the Ten Bells. *India.* For a moment, it felt to him as if he'd conjured her out of thin air by the sheer force of his longing.

She walked in, her leather doctor's bag in one hand, an umbrella in the other, water dripping off the hem of her raincoat. Her spectacles were fogged up. A sodden tendril of hair trailed down her slender neck.

A boy followed at her heels. With startled surprise, Sid realized it was Jimmy Evans. He barely recognized the lad. His face was scrubbed pink. His hair was neatly cut. He was wearing a clean set of clothes.

Sid had to stifle a smile at the sight of him. He remembered how badly Jimmy had taken the news that he was going to work for the doctor. If looks could kill, Sid would've been dead and buried. Now the lad trotted behind her like a faithful guard dog. She had that effect on people.

Even if Sid hadn't seen India's beautiful face, he would have known it was her. Buffeted by wind and rain, and likely exhausted at this late hour, her posture was still perfect, her purpose and passion evident in her every gesture.

He watched her, cursing his traitor heart, as she walked to the far end of the bar, found two seats, and wedged herself and Jimmy in between a pair of burly workmen. His interest turned to disbelief as she spoke to Benny the bartender, who disappeared into the kitchen only to reemerge with a pot of tea and two cups and saucers and placed them on the bar. A pot of tea in this shithole of a pub! Sid was half tempted to go ask the man if he could get a scone with jam. Benny disappeared again and returned with two plates of pie and mash. Curling plumes of steam rose from them as he set them down. India ate hers bite by neat bite. Jimmy tore into his.

Once you know hunger, you never forget it, Sid thought.

India was the only woman in this working-man's pub, with its bellowing and swearing, its sawdust and spittoons. Any other female would have been shown the door. Not her, apparently. She clearly wasn't a man, but she wasn't a woman, either. Not to her fellow patrons. How could she be? What kind of woman cut into a belly and pulled out a burst appendix? What kind of woman looked after shaking drunks and streetwalkers? These men knew her, respected her, loved her, even—though they never would have admitted it. She'd doctored their wives and children, delivered their babies.

Sid knew that too many doctors took their patients' pride along with their money, telling them all the things they should be doing for their kids—feeding them milk and meat every day, getting sunshine on them and fresh air in them. Meat on a docker's wages? Fresh air in bloody Whitechapel? It was impossible and everyone knew it, but still, it made them feel ashamed. Those doctors knew a lot, but not one of them seemed to know that it wasn't only rich people who loved their children.

Dr. Jones wasn't like that. She didn't lecture. She didn't scold. Oh, she used to. She used to hold up pictures of smiling apples and dancing carrots and talk about porridge, but now she listened more than she talked. She was the only one who did. The ministers and priests didn't. The teachers didn't. The bosses, neither.

That's why her patients loved her.

That's why he did.

He'd told her they were finished and he'd meant it. But the mere idea drew a bitter laugh from him now. He would never be finished with her. He would love her until the end of his life. Watching from afar. Watching as she opened her clinic in that tumbledown factory of hers. Watching as she found another man, a better man, and shared her life, her hopes, her heart, with him.

Jimmy, having scraped his plate clean, left India and made his way through the crowd of men to the loo at the back of the pub.

She was alone now, and Sid yearned to go to her. To talk to her. See her smile. See her eyes light up. As he stood there clutching his empty glass, hope got the better of him. It whispered in his ear, making him believe that even if they couldn't be lovers, they could still be something to each other.

Maybe she understands, the voice said. *Maybe she even agrees. She's had time to think it through. Surely, she sees the sense of it now.*

He put his glass down and started toward her. He didn't have to push his way through the crowd; men stood aside for him. But when he reached her, he saw that there was no room between her and the men on either side of her. Sid tapped the man at her left on his shoulder. He turned and looked at Sid, a belligerent expression on his face, ready to tell him where to go, but then his eyes widened and he smartly stepped aside.

"Evening, Dr. Jones," Sid said, as he took the man's place.

India had finished her supper. She was staring straight ahead of herself, her teacup halfway raised to her lips. She sucked in her breath softly and set the cup back in its saucer.

"Filthy night. Skies are throwing it down," he said. "Saw you come in. Didn't know you frequented the Bells. What are you doing out and about at this hour?"

He was babbling. Chiding. Talking about the weather like some barmy old dear. Finally he made himself stop, hoping she would say something, but she didn't. So he tried again, desperate.

"How's the boy doing?"

"Fine."

"Just fine?"

"He has a bit of a fresh mouth," she allowed. "And a very good mind. He needs more to occupy it than I can provide. Schooling, for starters."

"What are you going to do about it?"

"There is little I can do."

Sid saw that it bothered her. He wished he could help, but didn't know how. "I hope he's walking you back to Brick Lane," he said, just to keep the conversation going.

India shook her head. "He lives here now. Above the pub. With his siblings."

"Ah."

Another long silence ensued. Once again, Sid broke it.

"Haven't seen you since the day you smashed up *my* pub."

"That is an exaggeration. It was one window."

"You looked like you'd been through the ringer. What happened?"

"I fell."

Sid nodded, then he said, "What really happened?"

"I told you, I fell."

"India–"

"No one likes a snitch, Mr. Malone," India said curtly, still not looking at him.

Sid's eyebrows shot up. "Spoken like a true villain. We must be rubbing off on you."

He hoped to get a rise out of her, to keep the conversation going, but once again, it died. Whatever had happened to her was not for him to know. But he wished to God she would say *something*. The noise around them was deafening, but all he could hear was the silence between them.

"Talk to me, India. Please."

India shook her head. "You cannot have it both ways, Sid. You cannot end it with me and continue it with me."

"Can't we…can't we be friends?"

"I do not make a habit of sleeping with my friends."

India pushed her plate, cup, and saucer across the bar. Benny saw her do it.

"Another round, er…pot, Missus?"

"No, thank you," India said, reaching into her skirt pocket.

"Forget it," Benny said, glancing at Sid. "It's on the house."

"Thank you, but I wish to pay for my meal and the boy's," India said, placing a shilling on the bar.

The bartender looked at the coin as if it might explode. India insisted he take it. Sid nodded and he did. As he handed her the change, Jimmy reappeared from the loo.

"Ev'nin, Mr. Malone," he said.

"Ev'nin, lad. How are you getting on at the doctor's?"

Jimmy took a breath, preparing an answer.

Sid beat him to it. "Giving her a bit of gyp, I'm told."

"A bit," Jimmy admitted, dropping his gaze.

"I'm disappointed to hear that. It stops. Right now."

"Yes, sir," Jimmy said, shamefaced.

India stood; she picked up her bag.

"Where are you going?" Sid asked her.

"Home," she replied. "Good night, Jimmy. I'll see you in the morning."

"Good night, Dr. Jones. Thank you for supper," Jimmy said, his eyes jumping from her to Sid and back again. There was concern in them. But Sid didn't see it. His attention was on India.

"You can't walk home by yourself," he said to her. "It's not safe."

"Good night, Sid."

"India, you can't walk through Whitechapel at night alone!"

But India was already halfway to the door.

"India, *wait,*" Sid said, louder than he wanted to. With a muttered curse, he followed her.

The weather had improved, but the streets were still wet. Light from the gas lamps flickered on the rain-slicked cobbles.

"You're being foolish," Sid said as he caught up to her. "If you won't let me walk with you, at least let me find you a cab."

India whirled on him, her coolness gone, anger sparking in her eyes. "Oh, please do stop playing the big man. You are not a big man, Sid Malone. You're a coward."

Sid stopped dead, stunned. India turned and kept walking.

"What did you call me?" he shouted after her.

"A coward!" she called over her shoulder. "At the first sign of adversity, you turned tail and ran!"

"Do you think I wanted to do it? I made the only decision I could! And I didn't make it for me, I made it for you!"

"You have no right to make decisions for me," India shot back, still walking.

Sid ran to catch up with her. He took hold of her arm. "I'm trying to protect you, India! Don't you understand that?"

India shook him off and picked up her pace. "Protect me from whom? I'm not afraid of your colleagues, Sid. I thought I made that clear at the Bark, when I—"

"Damn it, India, you should be afraid! You—"

India stopped dead and faced him. "I am *speaking,*" she hissed, furious now.

Sid stopped, too. Anger rose in him, splotching his cheeks red, but he closed his mouth.

"You talk of how dangerous your world is," India continued. "But the dangers I face are real, too, and more deadly than Billy Madden or Teddy Ko could ever hope to be. Have you ever thought about that? On any given day, I risk contracting any number of dread diseases from my patients. Tuberculosis is the one that scares me most, but cholera, smallpox, typhus, typhoid fever, yellow fever, scarlet fever, measles, rubella, polio, influenza, and pneumonia are killers, too. And since London has ships coming in from all corners of the world, I can add dengue fever, lassa fever, malaria, and plague to the list. And then there are deranged or intoxicated patients. They pose a very grave danger, especially if they gain access to scalpels or scissors."

"India, listen to me—"

"No, Sid. *You* listen to *me.* There's a reason why I've given you this long and tedious list of my professional hazards. It is because I want you to understand that I know, better than most, how fragile life is. How quickly it can end. And how painful that end can be. But even so, I do not fear death. I fear life, Sid—a life without you in it. I fear a withered and loveless existence. Because I have known one." She swallowed hard. Silver tears shimmered in her eyes. "So no, Sid Malone. I do not want to be your *friend.*"

And then she was gone, hurrying up Commercial Street

alone.

Sid followed her at a distance as she turned onto Hanbury Street, and then Brick Lane, making sure she got to the Moskowitzes' house safely. Watching as she pulled a key from her pocket, unlocked the door, and disappeared inside it. Then he shoved his hands deep down in his jacket pockets and walked back the way he'd come. Angrier than ever. And heartbroken.

"Bloody woman," he muttered.

Calling him a coward, of all things. A coward! *Him!* Why, there wasn't a bloke in all of East London, not one, who didn't fear him.

She was infuriating. She was out of line. Full of cheek. High-handed.

And worst of all?

She was right.

Chapter 26

"India, Ella! Where are you? You have a visitor!"

India, sitting on the examination table inside the shed cutting old sheets into bandages, looked at Ella, who was sitting in a chair doing the same. The clinic was closed for the evening. It had been another busy Monday.

"Are we expecting a visitor?" she asked.

Ella shook her head. Both women rose and walked out into the yard and saw Mrs. Moskowitz standing by the chicken coop with a man in a blue uniform.

"Sergeant O'Meara, how lovely to see you again," India said warmly, as she and Ella walked over to him.

Roddy O'Meara smiled. "*Lovely to see you,* is not a greeting I'm used to hearing, Dr. Jones." He nodded at Jimmy, who was at the bottom of the yard hauling a dustbin out to the alley. "How is young Dr. Evans doing?"

"Young Dr. Evans is going to cost us all of our patients if he doesn't stop insulting them," India said.

Days ago, India had told Roddy a highly edited version of how she'd come to employ Jimmy, and to her relief, he hadn't pressed her too hard about the details. He'd been relieved that Jimmy hadn't come to harm, and happy that he'd been given an honest job and could provide for his siblings.

"You make jokes, Sergeant O'Meara, but this boy…he could be a doctor," Mrs. Moskowitz said. "He could be anything. He is very bright."

"He might just get the chance."

"What do you mean?" India asked.

"I received a visit from an attorney this morning. He had an envelope with him. It contained two letters; one for me and one for Jimmy. It also contained a bank draft and I don't mind telling you, I was gobsmacked when I saw the amount."

India's ears pricked up. Her heartbeat quickened. She and Ella traded glances. Something like this had happened once before when Sid had sent money to India for her clinic. Was he behind this, too?

"Is the money for Jimmy?" Ella asked.

"It is. I'm to manage it for him."

"What is the boy supposed to do with it?" asked Mrs. Moskowitz.

"I'll let him tell you," Roddy said, then he stuck two fingers in his mouth and blew a shrill whistle. Jimmy, back inside the yard now and wrangling a second dustbin, looked up. Roddy motioned him over.

"I didn't do it. Not this time," he said warily as he joined the group.

"You're not in trouble, lad," the sergeant said, pulling a letter from inside his jacket. "Here, this is for you."

Jimmy took it uncertainly. He looked at his name on the front of it, neatly typed, then turned it over, but there was no return address. "Who's it from?" he asked.

"I don't know," Roddy O'Meara replied. "Why don't you open it?"

Jimmy did so. Then slowly, he read it. When he finished, he thrust it at India. "Here…*here*!" he said, backing away. "I don't want it."

India, stunned by his reaction, took it from him. "What's wrong, Jimmy? What does it say?" she asked.

"It says I can go to a school for boys. In the country. And me, Ollie, and Alfie can move there. And someone with a long name I don't know how to say is going to pay for it all. Ana... Ano...I can't remember."

"Anonymous?" Ella ventured.

"I think so..."

"*Mazel tov!*" Mrs. Moskowitz exclaimed. "This is amazing, Jimmy! A miracle!"

"No, it's not, Mrs. Moskowitz! I don't want to go to the flippin' country! Or to school!" Jimmy cried, upset.

"May I read the letter?" India asked.

Jimmy nodded.

"It's true," India said when she'd finished. "An anonymous benefactor wishes to pay for school for Jimmy and his siblings and provide them with accommodations and an allowance. He asks Sergeant O'Meara to use the enclosed bank draft for those purposes."

"Anonymous, is he?" said Mrs. Moskowitz, in a tone that conveyed the benefactor was anything but.

"It's him, isn't it? Sid Malone?" Roddy O'Meara asked.

India folded the letter and slid it back into its envelope. Sergeant O'Meara did not miss much, and she did not want him reading her face. It would give away a good deal more than the letter.

"It has to be Malone. Who else around here has that kind of dosh?" Ella asked.

"It ain't him," Jimmy said. "Sid Malone wants to chuck me in the river."

"He's not the only one," said Ella. "How soon do you leave?"

"I'm not leaving," Jimmy protested. "I told you, I'm not going."

"Jimmy, this is an incredible opportunity. Of course you're going," India said.

"I'm not," Jimmy said stubbornly, then he stalked off back across the yard to the dustbins.

"He is frightened, that's all. Give him time. He'll come around," said Mrs. Moskowitz.

But India didn't share her optimism. She knew, all too well, just how obstinate Jimmy Evans could be. She went to him now, hoping she could talk sense into him. But he refused to look at her, keeping his focus on his task.

"Forget it, Dr. Jones. I'm not going. I'm *not,*" he said, dumping a basket of rubbish from the clinic into a dustbin.

"Jimmy, you would be mad to turn this down. The letter says your benefactor will pay for Ollie's schooling, too. And Alfie's, eventually. Think of them. You'd all have a proper home and the country air would be so good for Alfie's lungs. You can't possibly say no."

Jimmy, his eyes down, his face closed-off, shook his head. "I want to stay here, Dr. Jones. Working for you. It's a good job. It's money enough. We can survive on it."

"But you can do so much more than survive. You're smart, Jimmy, and now with this help, you can learn and grow and go farther in life than you ever imagined."

"Easy for you to say, Dr. Jones. I bet school was a doddle for you."

"No, Jimmy, school was not a doddle for me. Women are not wanted in medical schools. I was called dreadful names. Harassed mercilessly. Some of the male students tried to have me thrown out."

Jimmy stopped what he was doing and looked up at her. "Just for being a girl?"

India gave him a rueful smile. "For being a girl who got better grades than they did."

"But you're a toff, Dr. Jones. And schools are for toffs. Not for kids like me."

"That's an excuse, Jimmy Evans, a shabby one," India chided. "I expect better from a boy brave enough to climb up a drainpipe in the dark."

Jimmy's fearful expression hardened into a sullen one. "Yeah? Well, maybe you expect too bloody much."

And then he stalked off, disappearing through the doorway to the alley. India stared after him, defeated. She dragged the last dustbin out herself, then rejoined the others.

"Looks like that went well," Ella observed tartly.

"He is a very vexing boy," India huffed.

"I never pegged Sid Malone as a philanthropist or The Firm as a charity, not until you told me that he'd given you the money to renovate your factory, Dr. Jones," Roddy O'Meara said. "Why is he doing this?"

"I don't know, Sergeant," India said.

"Perhaps he's just trying to save a life. To do his little bit of good in the world. As we all try to do," said Mrs. Moskowitz.

"Save a life?" Roddy echoed, with a scoff. "Does Sid Malone really think saving one slum boy's life will make up for all the bad things he's done?"

Mrs. Moskowitz's eyes narrowed, just slightly. She smiled.

Oh, dear, India thought. She knew that smile; it was one Mrs. Moskowitz gave to people who didn't quite see things her way.

"Sergeant O'Meara," Mrs. Moskowitz said, "there is a saying I am particularly fond of..."

Ella snorted. "Only one?"

"...I will share it with you," Mrs. Moskowitz continued, ignoring her daughter. "It comes to us from the Talmud. *Whosoever saves a life, it is as though he had saved the whole world."*

She went silent then, letting her words sink in. Roddy O'Meara was holding his helmet in his hands. He looked down at it for a few seconds, his cheeks coloring a little, then he returned his gaze to Mrs. Moskowitz.

"I'll have to remember that one," he said.

"Do," said Mrs. Moskowitz, then she briskly changed the subject. "I never see you at our café, Sergeant O'Meara. Why is that?"

"Because there are more villains in your café than there are in Wandsworth Prison," Roddy replied.

"You might be right," Mrs. Moskowitz allowed.

"Doesn't it worry you?"

"Why should it? They are polite to my children. Respectful to my husband. They eat their food and go on their way. More I cannot ask from my customers."

"But your restaurant is very busy. The till must be full of money at the end of the day."

Mrs. Moskowitz smiled again, this time warmly. "I only ask these men to pay for their food, not to take my cash box to the bank," she said. "I am not a fool, Sergeant O'Meara. I know enough not to send a dog to the butcher shop. Come, now. It's almost closing time, but I still have some brisket left. Sit down and eat a little something. The villains will not trouble you if you do not trouble them. The lion can lie down with the lamb, no?"

"I suppose so, Mrs. Moskowitz. But when naptime's over, only one of them's getting up."

Laughing, Mrs. Moskowitz took Roddy O'Meara by the arm. "I like you, Sergeant," she said, leading him toward her kitchen.

India and Ella watched them go.

"That woman is too much. First, she lectures the man, then she turns him into a customer," Ella said. She looked at

India. "Are you going to go after Jimmy?"

India shook her head. "We have to let him make his choice, El. We can't do it for him."

"That's true. All we can do is hope he makes the right one," Ella said. She started back to the shed. "Come on, Dr. Jones, we have to finish making bandages for tomorrow. Ah, the endless glamor of the medical profession."

India smiled at her words, but her eyes followed Sergeant O'Meara and her smile faded. Roddy O'Meara was an honest police officer, and a good man—and Sid knew it; that's why he'd entrusted him with the funds for the Evans children. India didn't know how he knew, but Roddy had told her he'd met Sid, a long time ago. Perhaps Sid had taken his measure then.

Now, as she watched Roddy walk into the Moskowitzes' house, she felt a painful twinge of guilt. Once again, she had not been truthful with him when he'd asked her why Sid had helped the Evanses. She'd said she didn't know, but she did. Because she had asked him to, a few nights ago in the Bells. Not in so many words, but she had remarked that Jimmy was smart and that he should be in school, and now Sid had given him the chance to go. It was an incredibly generous thing he'd done for the boy, but India knew he'd done it for her, too. Because he wanted to be her friend and he thought this might be a way to do it.

But what Sid didn't understand was that she couldn't bear to see him, talk with him, be near him, but not be with him. What he didn't understand was that just standing beside him at the Bells, unable to touch his face or kiss his lips, tore her apart. The divide between their two worlds was too great for him, the chasm too deep. He was afraid for her. He'd said she was too good, too kind. Not hard enough.

And so she found herself marooned in a gray limbo, neither his lover nor his friend, with no idea how to move out of it. Was she just supposed to forget him? It was impossible. She might as well forget how to breathe. He was the rhythm of her heartbeat, the song in her blood. She heard his voice every night in her dreams.

Let him go, Indy... Ella had counseled. *...save yourself...*

India wanted to, but she didn't know how. She was far better at saving others. With a wistful smile, she thought of all the fairy stories she'd heard as a small child, about helpless damsels threatened by dragons and ogres, saved by brave knights in shining armor, then whisked off to a happily ever after.

"I could use one of those at the moment," she said aloud.

She started toward the shed to help Ella with the bandages, but as she did, an object lying on the ground outside of the shed caught her eye. It was Jimmy's dinner pail. He'd forgotten it. She picked it up, planning to put it on a shelf inside the exam room to keep it safe for when he returned.

If he returned.

A moment later, India was sitting with Ella again, cutting up sheets, worried about Jimmy, heartsore about Sid, and ruefully wishing that knights in shining armor weren't so thin on the ground in Whitechapel.

Chapter 27

"You're a daft bastard, a fool," Sid Malone said to himself, gazing at the train ticket in his hand.

What had he been thinking? She would never come. He balled the ticket up and was about to toss it into the rubbish bin, but before he could, there was a knock at the door and he put it down instead.

"Look what the cat dragged in, Guv," Desi said, as he ushered Jimmy Evans into Sid's office, a room on the first floor of the Barkentine.

Sid eyed him from where he was sitting, at a large round table with a set of old architectural plans for a warehouse at the St. Katharine docks open in front of him.

"He says he wants to see you," Desi explained.

"You forget how to say no?" Sid shot back, annoyed.

"Remember what happened the last time we gave this one gyp? Don't want any more bricks flying through the windows." Desi smiled as he spoke; his voice was warm.

He actually likes the little bleeder, Sid thought.

He kicked a chair out from the table, then nodded at it. Jimmy sat and Desi left, closing the door behind him.

"What can I do for you?"

Jimmy was holding his cap in his hands, fretting its brim.

He cleared his throat, then said, "I know you did it, Mr. Malone."

Sid leaned back in his chair and regarded him. "I have no idea what you're talking about."

"Someone's paying for me to go to school," Jimmy said, raising his eyes to Sid's. "And it's you."

"It's not. But it's nice of whoever is paying. Are you going?"

"I don't know," Jimmy said earnestly. "It's been two days since Sergeant O'Meara brought me the letter and I still don't know. I'm worried I haven't got what it takes. Bound to be a lot of toffs there looking down their noses at me. Telling me I don't speak right. Or dress right. Or eat my bloody soup right. Telling me I talk too much."

"If you ask me, it's the toffs who should be worried."

Jimmy put his cap on the table, and then his elbows.

"Make yourself at home, lad."

"Ta," Jimmy said, oblivious to the sarcasm in Sid's voice. "Can I ask you a question, Mr. Malone? You're rich, right? Bloody rollin' in it, I hear."

Sid raised an eyebrow, unhappy with the direction the conversation was taking. He was about to say so, but Jimmy didn't let him.

"So why don't *you* take some of your money and send yourself to school?"

Sid blinked at him, taken aback by the question. "I've been to school, Jimmy."

"I don't mean grammar school. I mean university."

"And what would I do at university?

"You could study medicine, like Dr. Jones."

"You must be joking."

"All right, maybe not medicine. Science, maybe. Or maths. Wait…I know! You could study the law! You must know every law ever written cuz' you broke all of 'em. Come to think of it, you could teach the course."

"You do talk too much, Jimmy."

"Why don't you, though?"

"It's a little late, lad," Sid said, surprised to feel a small ripple of sadness move through him at the admission.

"Yeah, I guess so. You're pretty old. But anyway, the reason I came here is to say thank you."

"I told you…it's nothing to do with me," Sid said brusquely. "You know who I am and what I do. I'm not a bloody Sunday school teacher."

Jimmy nodded. He went quiet for a moment, as if he was working up his courage, then he said, "You're doing it for me because nobody did it for you."

That cut close to the bone. Too close. "Are you finished?" Sid asked coldly. "Because I am."

Jimmy stood up, chastened, and took his leave. He started for the door. Sid watched him go.

"Oi, Jimmy…" he said, when the boy was halfway across the room.

Jimmy turned around.

"If you do go, do your best. Dr. Jones will expect nothing less. And that's one woman you don't want angry at you."

"Too right," Jimmy said with a laugh. "Guess if anyone knows that, it's you."

Sid cocked his head. The look on his face would have struck fear into the hearts of many a man, but Jimmy barreled on.

"I seen you both. Rowing like blazes," he said. "That night at the Bells."

"Jesus Christ, lad. Do you *ever* know when to shut up?"

"You upset her. In the pub. I saw it," Jimmy said, accusingly. "And then you ran out after her. You think I was just going to let that go? Not a chance. I followed you. From a distance.

You didn't even know I was there, did you? But I was all set to step in."

"Oh, were you now?"

Sid saw that Jimmy had the good sense to shrink a little at his tone, but he still didn't stop talking.

"Look, Mr. Malone, all I'm saying is this...she's no walk in the park and we both know it, but she's got the biggest heart. And nothing scares her. *Nothing.* Smelliest, crustiest, nastiest toe rag in all of London walks into the clinic, coughing, sneezing, dripping, spitting...and she don't even flinch. All she thinks about is how he feels, and is he in pain, and how can she make him better. She's the kindest person I ever met."

"Aye, that she is," Sid said, his voice suddenly gruff.

Jimmy slapped his cap onto his head. "You made a right hash of it at the Bells, but you should try again. Work up your nerve."

"Work up my *nerve?*" Sid repeated, in disbelief.

"Aye. Try flowers. Candy. Girls like that sort of rubbish. Ta ra, Mr. Malone."

And then he was gone.

Sid stared after him for a long moment. Then he shook his head and said, "Ta ra, Jimmy Evans. Take on the toffs. Take on the whole bloody world. Maybe you'll be the one to change it."

His eyes fell upon the train ticket he'd crumpled just before Jimmy had come to call. He reached for it and carefully smoothed it flat, Jimmy's voice echoing in his ears.

...you should try again...work up your nerve...

Sid picked up a pen, took a deep breath, and scribbled two words.

Chapter 28

"Here's a nice big pile of bills for you, Dr. Jones," said Ella, flipping through the envelopes she was holding. "Came in this afternoon's post. There's one from the chemist. One from the lumberyard. One from the surgical supply…the paint man… and one with no return address." She turned the envelope over in her hand, frowning. "That one's the builder, I bet. Probably thinks we won't open it if we know who it's from."

India, who'd been sitting in the shed at the examination table, writing up the patient reports she'd hadn't completed during the day, winced as Ella plunked the stack of envelopes down beside her. She leaned back in her chair, took her glasses off, and rubbed her temples.

"You look tired, Indy. Come and get some supper. The bills can wait."

"Thanks, El. I'll make a sandwich later. I should finish up here." She glanced at the stack of envelopes again and felt her heart sink. "The money's going fast, isn't it? And we're not even halfway through with the renovations."

Ella nodded. She started to leave, then turned and said, "You haven't heard anything from Jimmy, have you?"

It was Thursday. Jimmy Evans hadn't come to work since

Monday. He'd sent Ollie to tell them that he was sick. He was fibbing and they both knew it. He just didn't want to talk to them.

"I haven't. And I'm worried. You don't think he'd be foolish enough to turn the money down, do you?"

"So that he can stay here and lance boils? I hope not," Ella said. "Though I do think he'll miss us if he goes."

"Believe it or not, I'll miss him," said India.

"Oh, me, too," Ella agreed, laughing. "Without him, we'll have no one to tell Mrs. Robbins that her baby smells like cheese."

"No one to tell the Carter boy he could find work as a scarecrow," India added.

"No one to tell old Mrs. Lawson she could do with a shave."

India grimaced. "Maybe I *won't* miss him."

Ella promised to make up a plate for her and leave it on the stovetop. India thanked her and returned to her work. Two hours later, she had completed her reports. By then, dusk was falling, and for a moment she deliberated leaving the bills for the morning, but it wasn't in her nature to leave work undone, so she lit a lamp and dug into them, sighing as she wrote out draughts and debited the amounts from the clinic's ledger. Finally, she picked up the last envelope, the one with no return address on it. Ella was probably right—it was likely from the builder.

Steeling herself, she sliced the top of the envelope with her letter opener and pulled out a piece of paper. But it wasn't a bill; it was a train ticket to Margate—a seaside town, east of London—for Saturday, departing at 2:00 pm. It looked as if it had been crumpled and smoothed out again. Scribbled on it, in handwriting she recognized, was a very short message: *Come. Please.*

"Is this a joke, Sid?" she whispered.

Meeting her at the Great Eastern, making love to her, breaking it off with her, trying to be friends with her, and now this? A ticket to ruddy Margate? To do what? Stroll down the boardwalk? Buy some candy floss? Play ring toss on the beach?

Anger kindled in her heart, pushing out the sorrow and longing that lived there now. Anger at Sid for sending her this ticket, for not giving her room enough to even try to get over him. And anger at herself, for not wanting to.

She ran her hand over the ticket, wanting more than anything to write back. To tell him *yes*. To get on that train. But she would not. Because it would only make a hard thing harder.

India was just about to tear the ticket in two when a voice in the doorway startled her.

"Dr. Jones?"

"Jimmy!" she exclaimed, nearly jumping out of her skin. She hastily slid the ticket back into the envelope and put it down on the examination table.

"Sorry. Didn't mean to scare you. Can I come in?" Jimmy asked, not quite meeting her gaze.

"It's *May I come in?*" India replied, "and of course you may. I'm so glad to see you."

India saw that there was a pretty young woman standing behind him. For a moment, India didn't know who she was, then Jimmy stepped out of the way and India saw that she was holding a baby in her arms.

"Ollie?" she exclaimed, rising from her chair. "Is that you?"

"Hello, Dr. Jones," Ollie Evans said, giving India a shy smile.

Ollie was scrubbed and glowing. Her hair was neatly braided. There was a pleasing fullness to her cheeks. Her blue eyes, once clouded with worry, were clear and bright.

"I didn't recognize you!" India said, marveling at the

changes in the girl.

"It's my new dress," said Ollie, her smile widening. "I've got two!" she added, her voice dropping to a whisper, as if speaking her good fortune too loudly might make it disappear.

It's more likely good food and dry rooms, India thought, but she didn't say so.

"And how are you, little Alfie?" she asked, taking the baby's hand.

Alfie, mistrustful at first, shrank back against his sister, but then India's stethoscope caught his attention and he reached for the chest piece. India let him hold it, guiding his little hands to his chest, then she listened through his shirt. After a moment, she removed the instrument from her neck and handed it to him, using the distraction to give him a quick once over.

"His lungs are clear and his color's good," she said when she'd finished her exam. "You've taken exceedingly good care of him, Ollie."

Ollie flushed pink at India's praise, and India remembered that she was only twelve years old. She was so brave, so strong, it was easy to forget.

"Sit down, won't you?" India said, gesturing to a chair.

Ollie sat, holding Alfie on her lap. Jimmy remained standing. India leaned against the exam table and was just about to ask the children why they'd come by when Jimmy took off his cap and all in a rush, said, "We've decided to go, Dr. Jones. To school. All of us. Me and Ollie. Alfie, too. As soon as he's old enough."

India's heart swelled with happiness. A wide smile lit up her face. "Oh, I'm so happy to hear that, Jimmy!" she said.

"We're leaving London tomorrow," Ollie added excitedly. "We've got a house in the country. A little cottage. With a yard for Alfie and roses in it! Sergeant O'Meara took us to see it. It's ever so pretty. And there's a woman who will come and look after Alfie while me and Jimmy are in school."

"It sounds wonderful, Ollie," India said.

"Down!" Alfie suddenly declared, pitching himself forward, straining against his sister's arms.

"Stop it, Alfie," Ollie scolded, settling him back on her lap. Then she raised her eyes to India's again. "I'm going to study very hard,' she said. "I...I want to be a doctor one day. Like you, Dr. Jones. I want to help people like you helped us. So I can pass along kindness, like you said."

India swallowed hard, moved by the girl's words. "You would make an excellent doctor, Ollie."

"Alfie—" Ollie started to say, but her voice caught. She tightened her arms around her little brother and took a moment to gather herself. "Alfie wouldn't be here if it wasn't for you."

India put a gentle hand on the girl's back. "Alfie wouldn't be here if it wasn't for *you,*" she said. "All I did was identify the disease and prescribe medicine. You made him better."

"Down! Downdown*down!*" Alfie demanded.

Ollie wiped her eyes with the heel of her hand, laughing. "It's as if he's discovered his legs in the last few days. All he wants to do is walk."

"Why don't you take him into the yard and let him practice?" India suggested.

Ollie said she would, then carried her squirming brother out of the exam room. Jimmy didn't follow her; he remained where he was—standing in the corner, still clutching his hat, still not meeting her gaze. It was just the two of them now and an awkward silence had fallen. India was the one who broke it.

"You left your dinner pail," she said, taking it down from the shelf, a hint of archness in her voice. "When you stormed off the other day."

"You can keep it. Use it for a sick bucket. Might save the next poor bleeder who works for you from having to clean up a mess."

Poor bleeder? India thought, irately. She'd forgotten just how blunt Jimmy Evans could be. "Well. Yes, then. Thank you, I will," she said, briskly placing the pail back on the shelf.

Jimmy went quiet again, then all in a rush he said, "Look, Dr. Jones, I'm sorry for storming off and I'm sorry I didn't show up for days. I was trying to figure things out. Trying to make the right decision. It's hard, leaving the only life you know. Even if it isn't such a great one."

"It's all right, Jimmy," India said, mollified by his apology.

"I wasn't…I wasn't sure I wanted to do it," he continued. "I'm thinking it's going to be a lot of *Yes, sir* and *No, sir* and *May I* not *Can I.* I'm not sure I can do it, but I have to try. I don't mind telling you that I'm scared."

"I was scared, too, when I started medical school," India admitted. "I'm still scared most days."

Jimmy nodded, but his expression told her he didn't quite believe her. "Mrs. Moskowitz said I'll be all right. I saw her just now. Maybe I don't have a mum and dad, or a mansion to live in, but I'm still as good as any toff." He drew himself up straighter. "We don't get to choose our past, Dr. Jones, only our future."

India blinked at him, taken back by such a mature perception from one so young.

Jimmy saw her surprise. "Mrs. Moskowitz said that, too," he sheepishly added.

"You've made the right decision," India said. "You've been given an incredible opportunity. Make the very most of it."

"I will, Dr. Jones. I promise," Jimmy said. He squeezed his cap hard. "Before I go…I-I just wanted to say thank you for helping me. By rights, I should be in the nick. Instead, I'm going to go to school."

"I'm happy to have helped you, Jimmy, but it's not me who's sending you to school."

"I know that. It's Mr. Malone who's done it. I saw him yesterday, to say thank you. He wouldn't have, though, if it wasn't for you. If you hadn't come for me and faced all them villains down. Nobody's ever done anything like that for me, Dr. Jones. No one." He raised his head then, and his eyes found hers. "You forgave me. That's how you are. But Mr. Malone did, too. He forgave me when by rights he should have kicked my arse. I've been wondering why ever since and I think I know now. I think it's because he needs forgiveness, too. I think you should forgive him, Dr. Jones."

India was speechless. Did Jimmy know there was something between herself and Sid? How had he found out? She tried to cover her surprise, but Jimmy didn't let her.

"I followed you," he said. "That night at the Bells. I was worried. I could see he'd upset you, but he was sorry for it. You didn't see his face after you went inside, but I did. He looked angry at first, but then he looked sad. Like the saddest bloody man in the world. Don't know what he did, but maybe you should give him another chance."

"I-I can't…you don't…it's complicated…" India stammered.

Jimmy nodded, but she could see in his eyes that he didn't understand.

"Well, I've got to be going," he said. "A removal van's coming for us tomorrow, bright and early. Don't know why. We've nothing worth removing." He smiled then, as if something had just occurred to him. "Except ourselves."

India moved toward Jimmy, meaning to shake his hand, but instead of taking it, Jimmy threw his arms around her and hugged her tightly. "Me mum would've liked you," he said.

And then he was gone. And India was left standing alone in the exam room, with a lump in her throat.

It was getting late. She knew she should go to bed.

Tomorrow would be another busy day. But she remained where she was, her tired mind swirling with all the things Jimmy had said to her—that Sid had funded the boy's new life, that Sid was sad, that she should forgive him. She remembered their last meeting, and how angry she'd been, how cold, and her heart ached over it. But what else could she do? Sid would not let her into his world, and he refused to enter hers.

Her eyes fell on the envelope. She opened it and pulled the ticket out again. She heard Jimmy's voice in her head.

...he looked sad...like the saddest bloody man in the world...

India had been so hurt, so heartbroken, by Sid's decision to end their relationship that she couldn't accept his reason for doing it. Or see that his decision had cost him, too.

In her blindness, her arrogance, she'd thought that his world could never touch her. But it had. The bruises its harsh grip had left on her skin had faded, but the ones imprinted on her memory would last forever. She would never forget the despair she'd felt as the black carriage had made its way deep into the marshes. The gut-loosening terror of staring at the murky river water, waiting for Frankie to push her head under it. The shock of loaded guns pointed at her. That was what Sid wanted to protect her from. That was his world. It was dangerous. It was real. And it would not spare her.

She heard his voice now. *You're too good, too kind. You're not ruthless, and you have to be to survive in my world...*

Frankie Betts was ruthless, driven by a love of violence. So were Billy Madden, Teddy Ko and all the other crime lords. But India saw now that there were different kinds of ruthlessness. There was the kind that drove a frightened mother to bang on the Moskowitzes' front door at two in the morning, shouting for help, her sick child in her arms. The kind that drove a father down to the docks at dawn in his threadbare jacket to stand in the wind and the rain, desperate for a day's work. There was the kind that drove Jimmy Evans, who'd robbed her and risked a lonely grave at the hands of Frankie Betts to feed his sister and brother.

India put the ticket down, looked up, and caught sight of her own face, reflected in a small mirror hanging on the exam room's wall. She saw hollows in her cheeks. She saw shadows under her eyes. She saw weariness, put there by the long hours of doing the impossible, examining patients in an old shed, building a clinic out of little more than hopes and dreams.

And she saw something else, too. She saw that Sid was right: she would never become ruthless.

Because she already was.

It wasn't a criminal's ruthlessness she possessed, but it was every bit as fierce. No textbook had shown her that. No doctor, professor, or mentor. A boy had. Had she thought that there were no brave knights in Whitechapel? She was wrong; there was one. His manners were rough and his armor tarnished. He was mouthy and skinny and only fourteen, but he had come to her rescue nonetheless.

India tucked the train ticket into her skirt pocket. Then she doused her lamp, left the clinic, and started across the Moskowitzes' yard toward their house.

Right before she went inside, she stopped, looked up at the night's first stars twinkling so brightly, and whispered to them.

"Thank you, Jimmy."

~ Chapter 29 ~

Sid Malone paced the train platform, hands in his pockets, dread in his heart, stopping now and again to pull out his pocket watch, click the cover open, and check the time.

He had come to the station early. Hoping against hope that she would be on the train. But why would she? She was angry at him, deeply so. She'd made that clear the last time they'd met.

Finally, he saw the locomotive's nose in the distance making its way up the track. Why had he done this? Why had he sent her a ticket? Why was he here, waiting for this bloody train? He would be crushed if she wasn't on it.

The train pulled into the station and stopped in a whuff of steam, brakes screeching. Two conductors hopped off and made their way down the length of cars, opening doors.

A river of people flowed out of the cars: families arriving for their holiday, the harried parents, checking to see that they had all their belongings, their excited children already pestering for brandy snaps and toffee; courting couples in from the country for a fancy supper; gaggles of giddy teenagers eager to spend their hard-earned coins in the arcades.

But nowhere did Sid see the one face he was searching for, a face whose every plane and angle he now knew. Whose lips he yearned to kiss. Whose eyes he longed to drown in.

And then...there...*there!* Was it? It *was.* India. She had just stepped off the train and was smoothing her skirts. It was all he could do not to run to her.

"You came," he said, as he met her, reminding himself he mustn't embrace her, not here. He stood still, working to keep his distance, but failing to keep himself from touching her hand.

"I did, yes," India said, raising her face to his. "I'm not sure why."

"I-I rented a house," he said. "Out of town. Far away from everything. There are too many people here. I might be seen. You might be."

India looked down. He realized she had brought no overnight bag, only a small purse.

"Are you...are you not staying?"

"I didn't know you meant for me to."

"Will you?"

"I don't know, Sid."

He looked down at the platform. "Well, even if you don't... you've come, haven't you? Shall we take a walk, at least?"

India hesitated, then gave him a nod.

"Not here," he said. "Not in town."

She glanced up at the crowd of people thronging the platform. "No, not here."

"Joss Bay," he said. "It's not far."

Sid hailed a cab, told the driver where he wanted to go, then he and India climbed into it. The driver guided his horse out of Margate and east along the coast, arriving at the bay twenty minutes later. Sid got out, helped India down, then paid the driver. The man touched his hat, clucked at his horse, and drove off.

Sid offered India his arm. She took it and they started down a sloping path that led to a sandy beach. It was past five o'clock now, tea-time, and the bay was deserted.

"How's Jimmy Evans working out?" Sid asked, as they walked.

"Jimmy left the clinic to attend a school in the country," India replied. "He has a new home, too. His sister will also attend school. There's a woman to look after the baby, and plenty of money in a trust to fund it all."

"That's quite a turn of events."

"Oh, please. Don't bother," India said. Sid allowed himself a small smile. They walked on until they came to a battered old rowboat, turned upside down in the sand. Sid gestured to it and India sat down, facing the water. He sat next to her, then stared out at the sea. He heard the waves endlessly murmuring, smelled salt on the air.

"Is it wrong to want to help?" he asked.

"Everyone but yourself?"

Sid stiffened at her words, but did not reply.

India turned and looked at the side of his face. "You saved Jimmy Evans for the same reason you save all the other poor, broken-down wrecks you come across...because you cannot save yourself." She looked away again. "And you push me away because you think I might."

"I pushed you away because I love you."

"Of course. That makes perfect sense."

"I love you, India, and I don't know what to do about it," Sid said, standing. "I thought I did. I decided to see you at the Great Eastern...and afterward—"

India cut him off. "Yes, you decided. Because that's what you do, Sid. Because you're the boss, the guv'nor. So you make the decisions. But I'm not one of your underlings, and your decisions about me, about us?" She laughed derisively. "They don't involve me."

"Don't involve you? How can you say that? Since the first

time we slept together every bloody decision I've made has involved you!"

"But you don't ask what I want. You simply choose a course of action and I must accept it."

"You don't understand my world, you don't see the dangers—"

India stood now, too, and faced him. "Do not trot out that tired argument again," she said. "I *do* understand the dangers of your world, better than you could possibly imagine." Her voice faltered, but she gathered herself and continued. "You say I am not ruthless enough to survive in your world. But I am, and you know it. You're the one who's afraid, Sid. You're afraid of me. You're afraid that I'll try to save you and even more afraid that I'll succeed."

A silence descended then and the only sounds Sid heard were the breakers, the cry of a solitary seabird as it skimmed the water, and the beat of his own heart, smashing against his ribs.

After a moment, India broke it. "Take me home," she said.

Sid nodded. She would return to London. It was over between them. Forever.

"Trains leave on the half-hour," he said. "I'll look for a cab."

"No."

India took his face in her hands. She kissed him and he tasted the salt on her lips, and her wanting. After a long moment, she broke the kiss.

"Take me to your house by the sea," she whispered, resting her forehead against his. "You *are* my home, Sid. I will never leave you again."

Sid pulled her to him, burying his face in her neck.

They stood that way for a long time. In a sanctuary of their own making, where no one could find them and nothing could touch them. Sheltered by the scudding clouds. Kissed by the salt breeze. Serenaded by the whispering tide, endlessly reaching for the shore.

They didn't have long here, Sid knew that.

But it didn't matter.

All that mattered was this moment. This woman. This love.

We're here, he thought. *Now.*

Together in this place.

Where the sky touches the sea.

Where the world begins.

ABOUT THE AUTHOR

Jennifer Donnelly is the bestselling, award-winning author of 14 novels, including the books of the epic Tea Rose saga: *The Tea Rose*, *The Winter Rose*, and *The Wild Rose*, as well as *Molly's Letter*, a novella set within the world of *The Tea Rose*.

Jennifer's work has garnered numerous awards, including a Carnegie Medal, the Los Angeles Times Book Prize, a Michael L. Printz Honor, and has been named to numerous best-of lists from retailers, librarians, schools, and literary organizations.

Her books have been published worldwide, with her novel Stepsister appearing in 22 global markets. Five of her novels—*Stepsister, Poisoned,* and the Tea Rose saga—have been optioned for motion picture development.

Connect with Jennifer on Instagram, Facebook, YouTube and X at jenwritesbooks; on TikTok at jenniferdonnellyofficial; or join her mailing list at www.jenniferdonnelly.com.

Printed in Great Britain
by Amazon

51290102R00101